"I INTEND TO MAKE LOVE TO YOU BEFORE THIS DAY IS OUT . . ."

Ryan and Jenny stretched out across the huge bed, clinging to each other with all the longing that had built up between them ever since they'd met. Their clothes fell easily from their bodies, leaving nothing as a barrier and opening the way to the intimacy they sought. Ryan's mouth covered her breast, charging her with a burst of desire she had never thought possible. Why did this one enigmatic, bewildering man conjure up such fire in her? Jenny wondered. Why, after all the careful years of planning and building her adult life had he come along to effortlessly melt her into a pool of desire, wanting nothing but him . . . ?

DIANA MORGAN is a pseudonym for a husband-and-wife writing team. Residents of New York City, they met in a phone booth at Columbia University, and have been together romantically and professionally ever since. Their previous Rapture Romances are *Emerald Dreams* and *Crystal Dreams*. And as Melinda Helfer of *Romantic Times* says, "*Emerald Dreams* glimmers with a magical atmosphere guaranteed to enthrall and enchant the discerning reader."

Dear Reader:

The editors of Rapture Romance have only one thing to say—thank you! At a time when there are so many books to choose from, you have welcomed ours with open arms, trying new authors, coming back again and again, and writing us of your enthusiasm. Frankly, we're thrilled!

In fact, the response has been so great that we feel confident that you are ready for more stories which explore all the possibilities that exist when today's men and women fall in love. We are proud to announce that we will now be publishing six titles each month, because you've told us that four Rapture Romances simply aren't enough. Of course, we won't substitute quantity for quality! We will continue to select only the finest of sensual love stories, stories in which the passionate physical expression of love is the glorious culmination of the entire experience of falling in love.

And please keep writing to us! We love to hear from our readers, and we take your comments and opinions seriously. If you have a few minutes, we would appreciate your filling out the questionnaire at the back of this book, or feel free to write us at the address below. Some of our readers have asked how they can write to their favorite authors, and we applaud their thoughtfulness. Writers need to hear from their fans, and while we cannot give out addresses, we are more than happy to forward any mail.

Happy reading!

Robin Grunder

Rapture Romance
1633 Broadway
New York, NY 10019

AMBER DREAMS

by

Diana Morgan

PUBLISHER'S NOTE

This novel is a work of fiction. Names, characters, places, and incidents either are the product of the author's imagination or are used fictitiously, and any resemblance to actual persons, living or dead, events, or locales is entirely coincidental.

SIGNET, SIGNET CLASSIC, MENTOR, PLUME, MERIDIAN AND NAL BOOKS
are published by The New American Library, Inc.,
1633 Broadway, New York, New York 10019

First Printing, December, 1983

1 2 3 4 5 6 7 8 9

PRINTED IN THE UNITED STATES OF AMERICA

To Brian

Our favorite Berkshire mountain man

Chapter One

When Jenny first saw him, he was sitting, business suit notwithstanding, on a rock in the middle of the Housatonic River. His feet were covered by the flowing water, and the gentle rapids cut a path neatly around him.

Curious, she pulled over to the side of the road and parked in back of his silver Mercedes, staring at his motionless form. Although his back was to her, she could see that he was expensively and tastefully dressed and that the elegant pin-striped suit had been tailored with a fine and careful hand.

What did one say to a wealthy eccentric? Fortunately, she was in a good mood, and she was willing to take a chance. The delicate spring weather fairly bloomed around her, lifting her spirits, and the Berkshire Hills that bordered the valley seemed to rise gracefully right up into the clouds. It was Friday, and Jenny was looking forward to a week's vacation from her demanding job at the museum. The suitcase on the backseat of her car served as a pleasant reminder that today she would be leaving the museum early to be on her way to Cape Cod before five o'clock. With that prospect ahead of her, the thought of helping the obviously confused stranger in the river seemed like an amusement instead of an annoyance.

The car door slammed and she walked through the grass to the riverbank, but he made no acknowledgment of her approach. She hesitated, and then called out, "Hello? Are you all right?"

There was a pause. Then came a deep-voiced reply. "I've never been better." He didn't turn around, and she found herself addressing his back.

"Uh . . . what are you doing there?"

Still he made no move, but answered pleasantly enough, "Enjoying the view."

"I can see that," she sputtered. "But . . . but . . ."

"But what?" he prompted her. "But what am I doing with my shoes immersed in water?" He turned around at last, and she was startled by the laughter in his keen blue eyes. His angular face was marked with lines of experience that seemed to have been well-earned, and his reddish-brown hair was styled in a longish but conservative cut. Altogether he presented the very picture of sophisticated attractiveness—except for the fact that he was perched on a rock with his feet in the river. As if to emphasize this odd fact, he obligingly lifted his feet out of the water for a moment, watching with delight as the rivulets streamed from his dark brown leather shoes. Then he carefully placed them back in the river, smiling at her with an unmistakably smug air.

"But . . . why?" she asked, unable to conceal her curiosity. This was no lost tourist or local crackpot. This was an intelligent man of taste and refinement who didn't appear to have a screw loose.

The blue eyes assessed her for a second. "Would

you care to join me?" he asked. "It's quite soothing here. The water is deliciously cold, and the sun provides the necessary warmth."

She blinked. "Well, no . . . thanks. I'd really rather not. I'm late for work as it is."

He responded with a knowing laugh, to her further bafflement. "What's so funny?" she demanded. "Don't you believe in work?"

His laughter increased, and she frowned. "Forgive me," he said. "But I was just thinking how ironic it is. You're on your way to work and I just finished with work a few hours ago. Permanently."

She lifted an eyebrow. "Oh? You look rather young to retire."

A slow smile spread over his face and he nodded. "Thank you. You know, retirement has nothing to do with age. It has to do with one's freedom of position."

Jenny knew that he was gently toying with her, but curiously, she didn't mind. She faced him jauntily, her head cocked to one side. "Then this is indeed a coincidence," she rejoined. "I congratulate you on your triumphant departure from civilization."

This time he laughed as if she had just told a raucous joke. She smiled hesitantly, a bit nervous for the first time since she had greeted him. "I'm glad to see you're so amused," she continued coolly. "And now, if you don't mind, I think I'll just be on my way."

He nodded amiably and gestured toward her car. "Not at all. It was a pleasure talking to you." He sighed contentedly. "What a wonderful day this has been. It's only morning, and already I have enjoyed a beautiful view and the company of a beautiful lady. If this keeps up, I might be persuaded to stay here forever."

She didn't know if he meant here on the rock or here in the Berkshires, and she decided not to ask. He might be in need of help, but not the kind of help she had been going to offer. Backing away tentatively, she watched as he turned back to the expansive view, apparently taking no more notice of her. After one more quick glance at him, she got into her car and turned on the ignition. The motor sputtered a few times, rolled over, and then died, a cloud of smoke billowing out from under the hood.

"Oh, great," she muttered. "That's all I need." She tried again, but this time there was no reaction at all. "Oh, no. Please, God, not before my only vacation. Not today!" But it was no use. After pumping the gas till she was sure the engine was flooded, she sat back defeatedly and hit the steering wheel in frustration. "This can't be happening to me." Sourly she contemplated her ill fate for a minute, then looked over at the stranger, who was still perched placidly on the rock. "Say!" she called out. "If you're not too busy . . ." She let her obvious predicament complete the sentence, but he didn't even turn around. "Hey!" she tried again. "If you don't mind, my car won't start. Do you think you could give me a lift into town?"

A few seconds passed before he answered her. "I won't be ready to leave this rock for quite a while. Why don't you come over and join me?"

Jenny jumped out of her car and walked to the edge of the water, her feet making soft prints in the mud. "Now, look," she huffed. "I was kind enough to stop for you. The least you can do is reciprocate. I'm sure that rock will be there when you return."

"Can you drive a stick shift?" he asked.

"Sure," she answered. "But what . . . ?" She stopped as he reached into his pocket and flung a set of keys onto the bank.

"Take my car," he offered, turning back to absorb the view.

"Well . . . well, thank you," she gasped. "That's very generous of you." She paused. "But how will you get out of here?"

"Send a serviceman over for your car, and he can drive me into town," he said briefly.

"But what if he can't come right away?"

All she got for an answer was a wave of his hand, and with a shrug, Jenny opened the door of the Mercedes and climbed inside. If he was kidding, she was calling his bluff. She felt awkward at first, taking over this unfamiliar plush automobile. The bucket seats were covered in blue velvet, and the distinct smell of pipe tobacco permeated the interior. Sure enough, a fancy pipe sat on the dashboard. A leather attaché case sat on the floor, the name "Ryan Powers" printed in gold letters on the flap, followed by a Fifth Avenue address. Fifth Avenue, Jenny thought? New York City. Of course. She should have known. Like most of the local residents, she had a vague but strong distrust of people from the big city. To her, New York was a big, noisy, scary place, brimming with tall buildings, muggers, and fast talkers. This Mr. Ryan Powers was probably a stockbroker or a salesman of some kind. Well, if he wanted to lend her his car, she wasn't about to give him an argument. After sneaking one more glance at him, she adjusted the rearview mirror, snapped on her seat belt, and turned on the ignition. He never budged as she drove off.

The car was surprisingly easy to handle, especially as she negotiated the many twists and turns on the country roads. Only a slight depression of the accelerator and she felt as if the car were about to soar into the air like a jet plane. It purred powerfully as she steered, passing through the peaceful surroundings like a lion that had escaped from the jungle.

Although Route 123 would have taken her directly to the museum, she chose instead a smooth rural road that led through fresh flower-filled meadows. It was one of her favorite back roads, and she let the car coast along as she passed the two-hundred-year-old stone marker that pointed the way into town. There were no street signs here, nothing except landmarks to guide the traveler, and Jenny was familiar with all of them. The lovely setting calmed her as it always did. So what if her car had broken down? The inner restlessness that she had been unable to quite get rid of lately was put at bay as she maneuvered the Mercedes. It wasn't every day that she got to drive a car like this. She rounded a bend and downshifted, still impressed by its luxury, when she caught sight of a now-familiar sign that read "STOP THE CONDOS."

Jenny couldn't help but smile when she saw that sign, because she knew that soon it could be taken down—permanently. One short year ago the valley had been threatened by outsiders, but the residents had reacted swiftly and with typical Yankee ingenuity. It had been exciting, and because of her position as the head of the Josiah Akins Memorial Art Museum, she had been directly affected. The museum had once been the Akins family mansion, dating back to the days before the Revolutionary War, but the last occupant, old Josiah, had willed it to the town before his death. The land surrounding it, however, had been left to his two grandsons, neither of whom lived in the valley. They had remained conveniently absent—until last year. One of them, a T. K. Lester Akins of Houston, Texas, had contacted a land developer with the idea of building a huge condominium project on the land behind the museum. And that was when everything hit the fan. No one wanted to see the timeless serenity of the Berkshires marred by a parade of uninvited eyesores. Immediately the townspeople had leaped into action. Jenny, as director of the museum, was pressed into service on the committee. The development was a particularly ominous threat to her, because she had been planning to assemble authentic colonial houses on the land in question. She couldn't very well expand smack into the backyard of a condo dweller. A series of legal battles had ensued, and the valley had lost everyone of them. For a while it had looked as though nothing could be done, but the governor had come to the rescue at the last minute. The commonwealth of Massachusetts had offered to buy the land from the two Akins grandsons, and only last week T. K. Lester Akins had indicated that he was very interested. He was waiting only to hear from his lawyer, and then the deal could be set.

Jenny smiled ruefully. Now that it was almost

over, she realized that the battle had been a handy way to avoid confronting the restlessness that had been lying in wait all year. She had been glad to fight for her home, to stand up for simple good judgment and good taste. But now? Her smile faded into an unconscious look of discontent. Could the valley that had always been her home continue to hold all of the dreams and energy of a determined young woman ready to tackle the world? All she knew was that she felt a driving urge to break out and go somewhere, do something new. She had been putting it off for too long.

Her pleasant detour came to an inevitable end as the white columns in front of the museum came into view. She pulled into the parking lot and rolled into her usual space, mischievously hoping that someone would see her getting out of the fancy sports car. Sure enough, Margie Russo, her assistant, was entering the museum. Margie looked up and spotted Jenny, her brown eyes growing wide as she smiled at her boss.

"Coming up in the world?" she called out teasingly. "Did you rent it for your trip?"

Jenny couldn't help smiling back at Margie's round face under its mop of dark brown curls. She related the story of the stranger in the river as they went inside, climbing the stairs to her office, on the second floor.

"I don't know . . ." Margie laughed, shaking her head. "He sounds like a nut case to me."

"Actually," Jenny mused, "he seemed more overworked than eccentric. I guess that's New York City for you."

"You could be right. The hustle and bustle got to

him, and now he's permanently flipped." Margie grinned. "I hope you're not going to Cape Cod for the same reason."

"Well, you don't have to worry about that. As of this moment, I don't have a car to get me there." Jenny sighed and sat down at her desk. "What's on the agenda for today?"

Margie consulted a clipboard. "The usual. Budget problems, fund-raising letters, auction schedules, and . . . oh, yes, graffiti in the men's room." She smiled briskly. "What shall we start with?"

Jenny sighed again, barely able to conceal her growing sense of boredom. Even her pet project, the colonial houses that had taken shape behind the museum, was now finished, and the simple truth was that the excitement and challenge of her job had diminished considerably. There had been a time when, at the extremely young age of twenty-five, she had managed to single-handedly push and prod the sleepy small-town museum into a showcase that featured some of the most outstanding pieces of art in the entire region. She had combed tirelessly through attics, cellars, auction houses, antique shops, and even junk stores with the discerning eye of an expert. The tangible results of her efforts now filled the museum, her finest achievement. She had filled every room, even expanding on the land behind the building. Why should she feel so dissatisfied? Could she be ready to burn out at the ripe old age of twenty-eight?

Margie's eager face waited patiently for her to reply, but Jenny just couldn't face another budget report right now. These days, the budget was confined to the maintenance of the museum, now that the excitement of the hunt for each and every piece was over. There was no more room and no more money to expand any further.

Her eyes strayed to the windowsill, where a blue jay was pecking at a crumb, trying valiantly to pick it up in its beak. It hopped about, attacking the minute crumb from every angle, until Jenny felt like brushing the morsel with her finger into the bird's mouth. Finally she looked up dispiritedly and turned back to Margie's agenda.

"What about the budget?" she asked, forcing herself to sound interested.

"Well"—Margie ducked her head—"some of your calculations were a little off. I caught some arithmetic mistakes in one of the columns. You accidentally nicked a few thousand dollars off the allowance for the cleaning staff."

Jenny laughed weakly. "Thanks for catching that, Margie." She shook her head. "I never was good at math. Remind me always to use a calculator from now on." Her gaze returned to the windowsill, where the blue jay was still pecking away at the crumb. But as she stared at it, it suddenly gave up and flew off, disappearing behind the trees. Jenny threw her pen down and stood up. "Let's not worry about the budget this morning," she said. "Why don't you get started on those fund-raising letters, using the old ones as a model. I think I'll head over to the Whitaker House to check on the garden." Margie nodded, jotting down a few notes, and Jenny dug in her purse. "Oh, and if that stranger shows up, here are the keys to his car. I'll just leave them on my desk."

Somehow the day passed quickly, as the myriad

of details and daily problems caught her attention. The stranger in the river and her jumpy mood were both temporarily forgotten. Margie came and found her to announce that Bert from the service station had called and told her that Jenny's car would be dropped off at the museum that afternoon. It would be waiting for her in the parking lot, and she would be able to leave after all. Still the stranger's keys remained on her desk throughout the day, and as four o'clock rolled around he had yet to arrive. She was about to call Bert to ask him if he had picked the man up when Margie walked in with a look of mixed curiosity and anticipation on her rosy face.

"What is it, Margie?" Jenny asked. "You look like you've just heard a terribly racy joke and you're just dying to repeat it."

"Not quite," Margie answered dryly. "There's a very odd-looking man downstairs. I thought you should know."

"Odd? What's odd about him?" Jenny frowned.

"Well . . . he's just wandering around aimlessly with a sort of euphoric grin on his face. And he's wearing a gorgeous suit. He'd look great if it weren't for the squishy sounds his shoes keep making. He must have just tramped through a mile of mud. He's leaving muddy footprints all over the museum."

Jenny looked perfectly bewildered for a moment, and then her face settled in comprehension. "Of course . . ." she said, beaming. "It's him."

"Who?"

"That nut case I told you about this morning. He's probably come for his keys."

"Oh!" Margie giggled. "I should have realized. He certainly is striking."

"He is, isn't he?" Jenny smiled back. "I'd say he's one of the handsomest men I've seen in a long time."

"Thank you," said an authoritative voice in the doorway. They looked up to see the man in question standing and listening to them with obvious enjoyment.

Jenny bit her lip and ordered herself not to blush. So what if he knew what she thought of his looks? If he had been standing there long enough, he also knew that she had called him a nut case.

"Your keys are right here, Mr. Powers," she said smoothly. "Margie Russo, my assistant, this is Mr. Ryan Powers, the man I met this morning. He's . . . ah, celebrating his retirement."

Margie's eyes crinkled in fun, but his were instantly alert. "How did you know my name?" he asked.

"It's printed on your briefcase. In gold." Jenny tried not to sound smug.

"I see. Well, thank you." He scooped up the keys and dropped them into his pocket. "And now, how about my reward?"

"Reward? For what?"

"For bailing you out this morning. I don't lend a Mercedes out every day, you know."

"Oh." Jenny suppressed a sigh. Of course there had had to be a catch. "Well, what would you like?"

He folded his arms and leaned against the door frame. "How about taking me out to dinner tonight?"

Again Margie's eyes watched the interplay with

amusement, but Jenny maintained her poise. "I'm sorry. I'm leaving for a vacation immediately after work today." Her smile was cool. "How about a year's worth of free passes to the museum?"

His laughter was light, almost boyish, as he uncrossed his arms and strolled over to the window directly across from her. "That's really very generous of you, especially since I happen to know that admission to this museum is free."

"Ah, so it is." She nodded. Margie was standing behind Ryan, and she gave Jenny a huge silent wink, which Jenny struggled to ignore.

"Instead," he continued, sitting on the edge of her desk and looking down at her, "I'd like a guided tour of the museum. Right now."

Out of the corner of her eye, Jenny saw Margie's round face alight with amusement. She felt a sudden need to remain in firm control, and she looked up, facing him squarely. "I'm sure that can be arranged. Margie . . ." She peered around him. "Margie, call Edna downstairs and see if she's free. She's one of our best—"

"No," he interrupted. "You. I want a guided tour conducted by the curator herself."

Jenny couldn't think of a thing to say, and she looked down to avoid his gaze. Margie stood behind him, nodding emphatically at Jenny and lifting her hand in the thumbs-up sign. Glancing from one to the other, Jenny stuttered, "Well, I . . . I . . ."

No excuses occurring to her, and seeing there would be no help from either quarter, Jenny gave in. "All right, Mr. Powers. You drive a hard bargain. But I can only spare thirty minutes." She stood up and turned to go. As he followed Jenny,

Margie straightened up suddenly, wiping the hilarity from her face, and Jenny burst out laughing.

"What's so funny?" he asked amiably.

"Oh, nothing," she replied, sweeping past Margie and opening the door. "Come on, I think you'll like our museum."

"Have fun!" Margie called after them.

They took the stairs down to the first floor, walking together like two soldiers, neither one saying a word. But it was impossible to be nonchalant, because Ryan's shoes made little squelching sounds at every step. Jenny peeked, and saw the wavery water lines drying on each pants leg, just below the knees.

"I see you're recovering from your sojourn in the river," she remarked.

"Yes." He grinned broadly, just as they arrived at the first floor. A few people saw them and looked at Ryan curiously. He smiled at them as they continued along through the main hall. Squish, squish, squish.

Jenny whisked him into a large, sunny room on her left. "This is the Wingley Gallery," she announced. "It's one of our most popular rooms."

"I can see why," he answered as he looked around. The afternoon sunlight slanted ethereally through the high colonial windows, giving a light, airy feeling to the room. Paintings of New England landscapes and historical scenes were spaced at intervals on the clean white walls. He waited expectantly while she watched him out of the corner of her eye. Fleetingly she wondered why he had insisted on this tour. She was beginning to suspect that he had an ulterior motive, that there was far more to this man than he was letting on. It was too bad—she had to admit that she really didn't mind spending the time with him. If only he weren't so strange. She resolved to stay one step ahead of him.

He followed her to the other end of the room, where one large picture dominated the wall. It portrayed a group of Indians in a canoe, riding over perilous rocks in the middle of a river. She glanced at her companion, whose eyes lit up as he studied the scene.

"This looks very familiar," he mused excitedly, his eyes roaming over the canvas.

"It should. You were sitting there just this morning, enjoying the very same view."

"Ah, so I was." He nodded, noting the title of the painting. "*White Water on the Housatonic.* Of course. It looks like fun, doesn't it?"

"It is." Jenny smiled. "I know, because I've done it."

"You've canoed on the Housatonic? Sounds exciting. You'll have to take me sometime."

He strode on to the next painting, and she followed, slightly piqued by his attitude. It wasn't just that he was forward. He was so abrupt. But then, what could you expect from a New Yorker? She wondered just what it was he did—or had done, if she was to believe his tale of retirement—for a living, and finally asked him point-blank. He met her question with a cool gaze. "I evaluated various situations," he replied carelessly. "It was up to me to see that they were handled in an advantageous way."

She noted his use of the past tense. Maybe he was perfectly serious about retiring, after all. "You're . . . you were a consultant?"

His mouth smiled, but his eyes didn't. "Among other things."

She couldn't contain her curiosity. "Like what?" she persisted.

"Sometimes I played with other people's money."

"How, exactly?" She knew she was being a little pushy, but not any more than he had been.

He sighed. "I looked over their assets and advised them how to invest. I took small fortunes and turned them into big fortunes." He spoke casually, but the power implied by his words was not lost on her.

"You were a financial consultant," she concluded.

The humorless smile returned. "That and a few other things."

Jenny had the distinct feeling that it might not be wise to pry further, and she quietly led on through the museum. Although he seemed genuinely interested in the displays, she had the nagging impression that something else was on his mind. She led him quickly through exhibits of household items, including pottery, weaving, glass, early printing, and metalware. Jenny pointed out various things of interest as they went along, and he responded with perfunctory nods and an occasional question. She realized once again how very familiar all this was to her. It was no longer possible for her to judge the museum's impact on someone else. For all she knew, he was bored to tears by this whirlwind tour.

Suddenly his eyes lit on a collection of portraits in a far corner. With a firm hand on her elbow, he guided her over to it, muttering, "Well, I'll be," almost as an afterthought.

This was what turned him on? Formal portraits

of New England personages? They lined the wall in an even row. He stepped up to one that depicted a stern-faced man in an old-fashioned black suit. Jenny couldn't understand why this, of all the things in the museum, should stimulate his interest so avidly, but she obligingly hastened to provide a commentary.

"This is a portrait of our founder, Josiah Akins, surrounded here by pictures of his ancestors." His eyes seemed to twinkle as he examined the large, burly man in the painting, but he said nothing as he moved on to the earliest Akins portraits. He stopped again, lingering in front of one that was dated 1753, and studied it with a rapt expression. It was a stiff, formal pose of William and Martha Ramsey Akins, portraying the couple in an ornate eighteenth-century dining room. Ryan stared at it for a long minute while Jenny looked at him curiously.

"If you'd like to see the rest of the museum," she broke in quietly, "then we'll have to hurry. I plan to leave at five, and I want to come back to a clean desk."

She turned to go into the next room, but he remained riveted in front of the portraits. His dynamic, aggressive demeanor had relaxed into an almost contemplative pose. She reflected that no matter what he was doing, he always seemed to be brimming with life. Even now, his bright blue eyes were shining intently with some inner discovery. "Ryan?" she said softly. He turned and looked at her. His face was a little dreamy. "Let's go outside," she suggested. "I've saved the best part of the museum for last." He nodded wordlessly and followed her, stopping at the door to glance back one more time at the portraits.

She wondered nervously if she should have rushed him. If he liked portraits so much, maybe he wouldn't be interested in the colonial houses over which she had so painstakingly labored. But they were the crowning achievement of the museum, and though they had taken her two years to assemble, they were what most of the visitors came to see. She couldn't leave them out of the tour. She led him through the main hall to the terrace, which overlooked the neat row of houses that spanned the last two centuries.

He stopped and surveyed the scene, looking at the many tourists who were scurrying in and out of the dwellings. "Whose idea was this?" he asked, admiration coloring his voice.

"Mine," she answered as modestly as she could. "I can personally vouch for the authenticity of everything in them."

He strode ahead of her onto the path and stopped in front of the first house, an earthy cottage representative of the very first settlers. "The roof and sides were brought here piece by piece from Plymouth and reassembled," she said quietly, standing behind him. "Shall we go inside?" They entered, and he looked around, clearly impressed. "The spinning wheel was brought from England by the family that lived here, and even the dried corn husks were part of the original decor."

"You really should have a professional tour guide here," he remarked.

"We do have a few, but we could use more. Why, are you available?" she asked quickly.

He actually seemed to think about it for a few moments before shaking his head. "I'm not really qualified. I'd have to study up first." He said the words seriously, without a trace of his earlier teasing. Jenny didn't know what to say, so she led him outside and on to the next house, which was around a small bend.

"This one was built in 1832," she told him. She pointed out the simple but well-crafted furniture, the clocks and bound books, and the beamed ceiling. He nodded with real enthusiasm, and she silently scolded herself for being so pleased at his approval. She was the expert; she didn't need any plaudits from him. But there was something about his obvious intelligence and keen awareness that made her want him to appreciate her efforts.

She ushered him along to the next house, a Victorian farmhouse covered with gingerbread, then noticed that he was deep in thought. "Getting bored?" she asked quickly.

"No, no, not at all. I was just thinking how simple life used to be."

"Simple?" Jenny couldn't have disagreed more. "How can you say that? If anything, it was more complex. There were so many hardships, and everything had to be done from scratch."

Ryan nodded. "True. But people didn't have to put up with traffic jams, dirt, noise, crowds, machines breaking down, and irate people in too much of a hurry to appreciate what was around them."

His adamant tone surprised her. "Don't you think the people up here appreciate what's around them?" she asked.

He looked at her quizzically. "Do they? You're one of them, you tell me."

"They certainly do when it's about to be taken away from them." Now it was her turn to sound adamant.

"Invasion of the condos?" he guessed.

"How did you know?"

He shrugged. "That's not hard. It's the big topic around here, isn't it? I've seen several 'STOP THE CONDOS' signs, and everyone was talking about it at the service station."

"Well, something like that does make everyone appreciate things more." She pointed up at the hills. "Twenty thousand acres were pegged to make way for developers. Luckily, that's not going to happen. They were stopped in time."

"Were they?" His face remained expressionless, and she realized that he couldn't really care. This wasn't his home. Most likely he would come to his senses and by Monday be back in his office, looking out at blocks and blocks of skyscrapers. She showed him quickly through the Victorian dwelling and checked her watch.

"It's five o'clock, Mr. Powers. The museum is closing. And the tour has come to an end." They were standing in the parlor, and the late-afternoon sunlight was casting shadows on the flowered wallpaper. The room was quiet, and Jenny realized that they were the only people still in the house. She could tell that he realized it too, because he said nothing for a moment, letting the silence settle around them.

When he spoke, it was in a low, reflective tone. "Thanks for the tour," he said. "It was most instructive. A good way to begin my retirement." The reference to retirement took her by surprise, but she managed a weak nod. He chuckled. "I know you don't believe me, but you will. Today I'm beginning a whole new life."

"That's . . . that's very nice," she said faintly.

"From now on I'm going to live life to the fullest. Live for the moment. Take each day as it comes." His voice was still quiet, but his face was animated. He seemed quite sincere. "Starting right now, I'm going to do what I want, without worrying about the consequences." His face searched hers for a moment, and then, before she had time to respond, he took her soundly in his arms and kissed her. The kiss was short and intense—a firm pressure of cool lips, the merest hint of warm breath—and he gave her no chance to protest before he quickly followed it with another. This kiss was lingering, and he gently opened her mouth a bit, to impart a taste of spice and honey and promise. "What . . . what are you doing?" Jenny blinked, trying to catch her breath.

"I told you. I'm living for the moment. I'm doing just what I want to do."

"But what makes you think I want do it with you?" she demanded.

"Because you're nestling against me like a bird in its nest. Because I can feel your heart pounding through your dress. Face it, Jenny. I'm going to be around for a while. Don't make me wait. I'm not a very patient man."

She twisted out of his grasp and faced him, her face flushed but determined. "Maybe you're going to be around here, but I'm not. I told you, I'm going on vacation as of right now."

"No need to ruffle your feathers," he said calmly, watching as she smoothed her hair into place. "I love your hair," he continued in the same intimate tone. "It's the color of champagne. How long is it?"

Her hand flew protectively to the twisted roll that was pinned neatly to the top of her head. In truth, her hair fell all the way to her waist when it was loose, but she didn't want him to unpin it and watch it cascade down her back. "You're very sure of yourself, aren't you?" she asked.

"I am now," he agreed. "I didn't used to be, although everyone thought I was."

"That's very nice," she said, backing away, "but if you'll excuse me, I'm going to get in my car and drive off." He showed no sign of following her, so she added, "Feel free to stay as long as you like. Just close the door behind you." He nodded amiably and she turned on her heel and left, marching firmly up the path to the museum and feeling just a little foolish.

"Oh, Jenny!" She hesitated but finally turned back. He was standing in the doorway, his arms folded casually across his chest.

"What?" she called back reluctantly.

"Do you know of a cleaner's in the area that picks up and delivers within the hour?"

"No, I don't!" she shouted, peeved. "What do you think this is, Madison Avenue? Things are a little slower around here. Why don't you try washing your clothes in the basin in the pioneer house?" she suggested sharply. "That should be to your taste. Simplicity!" Pleased with her handling of the situation, she turned without another word and walked up to the museum.

The phone was ringing when she entered her office, and she picked it up without thinking. "Hello?" Margie came in and waited politely, but began to frown when she saw the growing look of dismay on Jenny's face. "Oh, no," Jenny kept saying. "Oh, no." She nodded a few times, her hand moving unconsciously to her forehead, and hung up the phone with a defeated sigh.

"What is it?" Margie asked, unable to repress her curiosity.

"That"—Jenny gestured to the phone with finality—"was the mayor. It seems we have had victory snatched from our jaws just when we thought it was ours to keep."

"What are you talking about?" Margie asked.

Jenny sat down heavily and grimaced. She looked up at Margie, who appeared thoroughly confused. "The land deal. Apparently the commonwealth of Massachusetts has been flatly turned down by T. K. Lester Akins. He got word from his lawyer, who advised against the sale." She watched as Margie's face crumpled. "Not only that, but it seems we're back to base one. Mr. Akins has a sudden hankering to live here. In condo heaven."

Jenny's words were met by grim silence, but at last Margie said, "It's not over yet. They just don't know whom they're dealing with."

"I can't believe this is happening today, of all days," Jenny muttered. "Just when I was about to leave for a week of uncluttered oblivion."

"Why don't you leave right now, Jen? Go ahead. Nothing's going to change before you get back. Go on and have a good time."

Margie's voice was encouraging, but Jenny shook

her head. "I wish that were true. But I can't leave with this on my mind. Not before I make about twenty-five phone calls, anyway. The committee has to decide what to do."

They quickly went to work as the sun disappeared behind the hills, and soon Jenny lost all track of the time. Between the two of them, they managed to reach all of the key people involved in the town, and a tentative meeting date was scheduled. After putting down the phone for the last time, Jenny fell back in her chair, overcome by fatigue.

"I'll never make it to Cape Cod tonight." She sighed. "I'll have to leave tomorrow morning. What time is it, anyway?"

"Almost seven."

"Almost seven! That settles it. I'm going home, Margie. There's nothing more we can do tonight. Why don't you . . . ?" She stopped, noticing that Margie was looking at the window, her face a mixture of puzzlement and alarm.

"Look!" Margie exclaimed, pointing. "Do I see smoke, or am I going crazy?"

Jenny jumped up and ran over to the window. Sure enough, a curl of smoke was coming out of the chimney of the pioneer house. And she knew just what was causing it!

"I don't believe him!" she cried, throwing her hands up.

"Who?"

"That maniac from New York." Without explaining further, she ran down the stairs and out the door, scurrying up the path to the pioneer house. She already had an inkling of what to expect, but when she opened the door, the scene that greeted her almost left her speechless.

Ryan Powers was seated in the rocker next to the fireplace, calmly stirring the contents of a cast-iron pot with a large wooden spoon. He nodded cordially as she gasped in surprise, as if he knew just what was causing her so much alarm. It wasn't just his audacity in being here, and it wasn't his casual use of the priceless antiques. It was the fact that he was fully attired in authentic minuteman's clothing, complete with musket and sword. His business suit was hanging up to dry on one of the rafters, and a tantalizing aroma wafted forth from the pot on the fire. He looked quite at home sitting there by the hearth, as if he had moved in and planned to stay.

Jenny found her voice and stepped inside, her eyes sweeping over the incongruous scene. "What . . ." she choked, "what on earth do you think you're doing? What is the meaning of this?"

His smile was guileless and his blue eyes lit with genuine friendliness. He pushed a shock of reddish-brown hair back off his forehead and turned to her with boyish delight. "Simplicity!"

Chapter Two

Jenny remained aghast at the scene. "You've got to be kidding!"

"On the contrary. I've never been more serious." Standing up and bending over the pot, he lifted the spoon and took a taste, squinting critically. "Mmmm," he breathed, savoring a morsel. "Delicious." He looked up at Jenny, who stood frozen. "Care to try some?"

"No, I don't care to try some!" she repeated savagely. "I would appreciate an explanation. You are trespassing and you are vandalizing the property of this museum. Don't you realize that you are on private property?"

"On the contrary." He sat down calmly and went back to stirring without reacting to her outburst, as if he didn't have a care in the world. "As a matter of fact, this is a public museum. Admission is free."

"I don't care if it's free or not," she hissed. "It's after hours. The museum is officially closed."

"Oh, good. Then we won't be disturbed during dinner."

"Dinner!" she shrieked. "And what do you mean, 'we'?"

"Well, I bought enough food for both of us. I

assumed you'd be delighted to sample my historic cuisine. Look what I have," he continued, picking up a yellowed sheaf of papers. "This was written down over two hundred years ago. It's a collection of recipes put together by Sarah Akins and it's been handed down through the generations. The dishes sound delicious."

She could only stare in dumbfounded outrage.

"You know," he went on blithely, "you should have them republished and sell them as a gift item in your souvenir shop." She remained silent as he flipped through the pages, but he ignored her manifest disapproval. "Rock Cornish hen with currant sauce, glazed ham, spiced apples, Indian pudding, baked squash . . ." He stopped for a moment to check his own cooking, giving the pot a good stir.

"What are you cooking there?" she asked faintly.

"Old-fashioned beef stew. And I've got a cornbread ready to go into the oven."

"Oh."

He leaned over and tried to pry open the door to the small oven. It creaked perilously on its hinges, and he stopped.

"It will open," she said. "I personally saw to every single thing in this house. Everything is in working order. Just . . . just use a little muscle." She couldn't believe she was advising him, but the whole scene was somehow seductive. She felt as though she really had gone back in time, to become the mistress of a working kitchen, rather than a preserver of interesting but no-longer-useful artifacts.

He went back to prying the little door open, swinging it back and forth to loosen it. When he was satisfied, he put his hand inside but withdrew it immediately. "Ouch! That's hotter than I thought."

"Of course," she replied serenely. "As I said, everything here is in working order. I must say, you're doing very well. Dinner will probably be ready just as the police get here. Shall I invite them to stay?" He looked up sharply and she smiled in teasing reassurance. She should be furious with him, she knew, and yet there was something about him that made her want to go along with his antics.

"Would you like to sit down?" he asked politely.

"Thank you. I think I will." She sat on one of the handcrafted wooden chairs, looking around apprehensively. She knew that she wasn't going to turn him in, but how far could she let him go with this?

He was busily going through the contents of a large grocery bag that sat on the table, taking out apples, sugar, cinnamon, and a stick of butter. An open bag of flour already sat next to a jar of molasses, a bag of cornmeal, and the pan of cornbread.

He looked over his supplies. "Do you think you could make an apple pie?" he asked. "I'm afraid I'm not as much of a cook as I thought."

"Oh, all right," she sighed, getting up to join him. "I can see you have all the ingredients."

"There's a rolling pin in that drawer," he said helpfully. "And a—"

"I know where everything is," she interrupted. "You forget, I put everything here. I bought, found, or bid for every item in this house." She paused. "Including that outfit you've got on."

He smiled and bowed elaborately. "Glad you like it. Now you're getting into the proper spirit."

"I must say, it looks very good on you," she said,

measuring flour and butter into a bowl. "In fact, I'd almost say you look familiar." She frowned searchingly. "I haven't seen you before, have I?"

He shook his head. "I doubt it. I've never been here before."

"Still," she persisted, looking at him carefully, "in that outfit, I could swear . . ."

"Well, it doesn't matter, because you're going to get to know me," he said cheerfully, watching her mix the dough. "I've decided to live here."

Her hand stopped in midair. "Here?" she repeated. "Do you mean in Great Barrington or in this house?"

"I'm not sure yet," he teased, but she only shook her head.

"You can't keep this up, you know," she said. "It's crazy."

"Not really. I've done crazier things in my life. Certainly less healthy things."

She nodded. "Like sitting in the freezing Housatonic River in your suit at nine in the morning."

"Now, that's where you're wrong. That was easily the sanest thing I've ever done, and definitely the healthiest." He went over to check the stew and lifted a chunk of meat on the spoon. "Here," he said, "have a taste."

She opened her mouth obediently and licked the gravy from the edge. "Not bad."

His eyes gleamed. "Wait till you taste the cornbread," he promised. "I followed the recipe exactly, or rather, as exactly as I could. 'Butter the size of an egg' isn't exactly a definitive measure."

Jenny laughed. "That's how they worded recipes

in those days." She watched him as he tried to clean a squash. "Here, let me do that." She glanced out the window and noted that the last rays of the sun were casting a long glow over the countryside. Here inside the house, the fire was creating most of the light, illuminating their faces but leaving the corners of the room in deep shadow. It was so easy to pretend that this really was the seventeenth century and that this house belonged to her. And it was fitting that she should enjoy it in this way. She had labored to create it, and now that the project was complete, she was savoring the results by experiencing them to the utmost. She was living a historical fantasy, watching the problems of the day vanish in the cracking fire.

"I have to admit," she said, beginning to peel the apples, "this really is very pleasant. I'd like to spend my entire vacation living here in this house, peacefully enjoying the rigors of pioneer life."

"Why don't you, then?" he suggested calmly. "I'll stay here and we can be the perfect colonial couple." She glanced at him, an eyebrow raised, but he went on cheerfully, "We'll get you a costume and let people watch us living in another century. It's not really even such a crazy idea. They do just that at Williamsburg."

"I have thought about it," she admitted. "It's just that we don't have enough room." A shadow crossed her face. She was thinking about T. K. Lester Akins' last-minute decision to turn down the offer from the commonwealth, but she immediately ordered herself to dismiss it.

But Ryan pursued the subject. "Sure you do.

You've got all that room in the hills behind the museum."

"I wish I did." This time she could not hide her dismay, and he was instantly alert.

"What is it?" he asked.

"It's nothing," she answered with a vague wave of her hand. She didn't want to tell this stranger all the problems of the valley. "I was just thinking about how my vacation was delayed, and—"

"No you weren't. You were thinking about something very frustrating. Why don't you tell me about it?"

She relented, rolling out the pie dough and shaping it deftly with her fingers. "All right. You win. But I'm not sure you'll want to hear about it."

"Trust me." He grinned.

She told him the whole story—Josiah Akins, the two grandsons, and the twenty thousand acres. She recounted everything, right up to the phone call from the mayor telling her of T. K. Lester Akins' sudden refusal. "So you see," she concluded, "it's all over. It's their land and they can do what they want with it."

"Yes, they can do what they want," Ryan said softly, "but that doesn't mean it's all over." He sounded so confident that for a moment she almost believed him. She looked up quickly and saw amusement dancing in his eyes. But he was staring at the fire, not at her, and she went back to slicing the apples into the pie. "You know, Jenny," he went on, "I did some asking around town today. About you."

"Oh?" This time her glance met his directly, and he nodded.

"That's right. They say you're Great Barrington's leading lady."

"Who says that?" she demanded.

"Everyone," he hedged.

"Well, they're exaggerating, whoever they are. I'm just a simple country girl, born and bred."

"Is that so? For a simple country girl, you've got more drive than a stockbroker trying to unload a stack of bad bonds."

She threw down her knife, annoyed. "That's a lovely analogy," she said dryly. "Only an uptight, overworked, hard-driving, money-grubbing New Yorker could put it quite that way."

His boyish laugh echoed around the small room. "Well said. I couldn't have put it any better. But I was merely trying to point out that you and I have some qualities in common."

Her face fell. "What? Like what?"

"The main one is that we both want out."

She stared at him, the apples momentarily forgotten. Had this unpredictable stranger read her mind? How could he know? How could he possibly know? "Out of what?" she asked weakly.

"You obviously want out of this place." He didn't bat an eye.

"Is that so?" She tried to sound very cool, but could only manage a false note of gaiety. "And just where do you think I should go?"

He shrugged. "That's entirely up to you. But New York might be a good place."

She could only stare at him as if he had just suggested that she catch the next spaceship to Mars. "You . . . you can't be serious," she spluttered. "I don't like New York at all."

"Have you been there?" he asked mildly.

"Of course," she huffed. "I've been to the museums. It's a big, noisy, dirty city, and everyone rushes around without looking at anyone else."

"Oh." His tone was sardonic. "Well, I guess you know all about it."

"What's the matter?" she asked in astonishment. "I thought you didn't like it there either!"

"My reasons are strictly personal," he said. "Just because I burned out there doesn't mean it's not for everyone." Suddenly he smiled. "But from what I heard about you and the way you put this museum together, this little town may be too small a pond for a prize fish like you."

"Maybe so," she allowed, "but right now this Akins character is making waves in my little pond. I'm not going anywhere until it's all settled."

"Oh, you'll take care of him," he said lightly.

"Don't be so sure. How are we going to convince a man who wants to make millions that he should settle for thousands?"

Ryan smiled, looking at her in a way that took her breath away. His charm was almost magnetic. "Don't worry about that," he said soothingly. "Right now he's a million miles away, in a future century. And I have something here that will definitely take your mind off him." He rummaged around in the shopping bag and produced a bottle of champagne, still cold, and two crystal champagne glasses.

Jenny's eyes sparkled with delight. "Now you're talking," she said happily, laughing in spite of herself.

He uncorked the bottle with great ceremony and poured the champagne carefully into the glasses. "I don't know what sort of wine is supposed to go with beef stew and cornbread," he joked, "but I have always believed that champagne goes with everything." He lifted his glass in a toast. "To simplicity."

She raised her glass and clinked it against his. "Simplicity." They drank, and the gently provocative liquid descended gracefully through her body, making her tingle with pleasure.

"I believe dinner is ready," he said, peering into the pot over the fire. "Shall we?"

The stew was delicious, and Jenny relished the feeling of eating it in this setting. Ryan cut squares of cornbread, letting the steam rise from it as he refilled their glasses. The tempting aroma of Jenny's apple pie baking floated through the room.

"You're not a bad cook at all," Jenny remarked after a peaceful minute had passed. "My compliments to the chef."

"Thank you," he said sincerely. "I rarely cook. Usually I eat out."

"Another one of your urbane habits?"

He swallowed some champagne. "Oh, knock it off, Jenny. You sound like a country bumpkin."

"Well, you're the one who wants to retire here," she retorted defensively. "Why did you come here, anyway?"

"I told you. I decided I'd had enough of the hustle and bustle, and drive for success. All the pushing and shoving and competition and all the things that made me a millionaire finally got to me."

"Then why do you defend them?"

"Because they're what makes the world go round. I merely overdosed."

She sat back and studied him. "And that's why you were sitting in the river this morning?"

"No. It was because I caught the sunrise."

"What?" She searched his face to see if he was teasing her, but he was perfectly serious. "You caught the sunrise? What happened, you couldn't sleep?"

He shook his head grimly. "No. I overworked." He poured more champagne and dished out the last of the stew before continuing. "I've got a gorgeous apartment on Fifth Avenue overlooking the park, but I never seemed to spend any time there. I wasn't there last night. Last night I never even went to sleep." He paused for a moment and smiled. "Now I'm glad I didn't. Otherwise I wouldn't have met you and we wouldn't be having this adventure."

She avoided his gaze and pressed him to continue. "If you weren't at home last night, where were you?"

"In my office." He sighed. "That's where I usually am. It's on the seventy-seventh floor of the World Trade Center, which is a completely self-sufficient building. It's constructed so that no one who works there ever has to leave it, and sometimes I don't come out for very long stretches of time."

She stared at him curiously, noticing for the first time that his face was a little drawn and his eyes were rimmed with red. "Like last night?" she guessed.

"Right. The symptoms of a true workaholic." He drained his glass and refilled it, sipping hungrily. "I was going over the portfolio of a client, and it had to be done fast. He was up against a deadline, and the challenge was like a shot of adrenaline to me. I drank several pots of coffee, slaving away like a fiend." He stopped, smiling in a detached way. "It was a night like many other nights. Except this time something was different." He paused again, and she said nothing to break the silence. "You see, I had no idea that I had been up all night. Day or night—it never made any difference to me. But when I finished with this portfolio, I got up and went over to the window and got the shock of my life."

"What was it?" She felt her eyes widen with fascinated curiosity.

"The sun," he answered with simple wonder. "The sun was rising in the east. I realized that I had been working all night, and now the sun was coming up." He took a long draft of champagne. "Sunrises are beautiful, Jenny, but they're not meant to be seen from office windows at five o'clock in the morning. Suddenly I felt as if my whole life had been spent in that office, while the rest of the world passed me by. So I did the first truly smart thing I've done in years. I stood up, left the building, got into my car, and drove and drove without thinking where I was going. My mind was on automatic pilot, and the car just kept driving. Eventually I got off the highway and wound through some country roads until I came to the bridge over the Housatonic. Somehow I knew that that was the place to stop. So I did. I stopped the car and looked at the river flowing by so peacefully, and I knew what I had to do next. I just walked right into that river and sat down on that rock. And that was where you found me."

"That was where I found you," she echoed, "and somehow, I'm not surprised."

A long moment passed between them as they looked at each other, sharing that memory. The kisses they had shared earlier in the day came back to her suddenly, and unbidden, a thread of desire found its way into her blood. She hid her face behind her champagne glass.

"I . . . I think the pie is ready," she said. "I'll go check." She stood up, glad for something to do, and peeked inside the little oven. The top of the pie was nicely browned, and the apple juices were bubbling golden brown at the edges. Ryan came up behind to look, then reached inside with a cloth draped over his hands. He placed the pie on the wooden table, and they both admired it.

"You're a good pastry chef," he observed.

"Thank you."

All at once Jenny knew that they had run out of words and he was going to take her in his arms. He felt very warm and near as she turned to him, and his eyes were dancing in the firelight. Once again he looked fleetingly familiar, but of course that was impossible. Her last thought before he gathered her close and centered his warm mouth on hers was that anything was possible in this unearthly setting. He was a rebellious revolutionary, and she was the proprietress of this homespun cottage.

She did not resist him, at first because it was so easy to give in to this fantasy, but then because her response flew up within her with a sudden rush that took her by surprise. His mouth tasted warm and sweet and there was something about the way his strong arms circled her so decidedly that made her welcome his pursuit. The first kiss lasted for a long, enticing minute, while their tongues met in a silky little battle. Jenny's back arched and her head fell back as he began to leave a fiery trail on her neck, moving down to her throat to the tender hollow where her pulse throbbed. Every touch left a tiny pool of sensation that fed the river of longing flowing down the length of her body. Surrender seemed so easy, here in the firelight with this magnetically attractive man. So easy to pretend, to lose herself in his power, to let her responses soar. His fingers strayed to the buttons on her dress, effortlessly undoing them as they found their way to the softness inside. She clung to him, her eyes opening and then closing again as his restless hands roamed over the curves of her body, exploring and claiming them for his own.

The eighteenth-century shirt he wore was open wide at the collar, making it easy for her to slip her hands beneath the fabric. His chest was broad and smooth and hard, and she could feel his sharp intake of breath as she let her thumbs tease and stroke lower and lower, while her fingers massaged his shoulders. Again she marveled at how easy this was. They had begun their intimacy without words, and none were needed. Her body was singing for him, completely honeyed by his advance, without cajoling or artifice. His hands blazed a path possessively over the small of her back, around the fullness of her hips and up the supple round of her stomach. A low, wanton sigh of pleasure escaped her, inflaming him further. His hands splayed across her breasts, claiming them both at once, then narrowed in to focus on the sensitive peaks that rose ardently at his demand.

Now they were both transported, shutting out the rest of the world to feast only on each other. The currents of desire that rocketed through Jenny's blood made her breathing grow ragged, her knees grow weak. She leaned against him, suddenly unable to support her own weight. His left arm held her fiercely while his right arm continued to travel hungrily around the silky firmness of her breast.

At long last he stopped and looked at her, eyes half-closed, weak with desire. "Come," he whispered softly. He led her to the double bed in the corner. It was a bed that had not been used for a long, long time, but tonight they would make up for the neglect. Jenny stretched across it diagonally, letting a secret smile dart across her face.

"What is it, Jenny?" he asked.

"Oh, I was just thinking . . ."

"Yes?"

"Of all the people who have made love on this bed, and what they would have thought if they had known that someday we would be here now, like this . . ." Her voice trailed off again.

He smiled slowly. "Just think of yourself as a part of history." His eyes became a fiery blue as he looked at her, stretched out languidly and waiting for him, and he lost no time in easing her dress down her shoulders. She sat up halfway to help him, letting it slip over her hips. Now she was clad only in lacy white underwear that barely covered her small round breasts and skirted her hips. Her wheat-colored hair had long since fallen in disarray, tumbling over her shoulders in defiant abandon.

She looked back at him and had to smile. She was looking at a minuteman ready to spring into action, but not the sort of action that revolutionary soldiers had been trained for. Awkwardly she removed the loose white shirt, letting her fingernails rake lightly down his chest before she fumbled at the unfamiliar clasp of the gray breeches. "I'm afraid I haven't done this for a few hundred years," she joked.

"Neither have I. But don't make me wait another hundred years. I want to make this a very long, slow evening."

She nodded breathlessly, catching the decided glint in his eyes. They were so very blue, and they shone with a brightness that struck her once again as being somehow familiar. He caught her stare and her hand at the same time.

"Here, let me do that."

She continued to gaze at him raptly. "I can't get over the feeling . . ."

"What?" The eighteenth-century buckle surrendered under his deft fingers.

". . . that I know you already."

He drew her close very slowly, savoring the delicious feel of her silken skin against his chest. "It's probably my job," he murmured, dropping several soft, tantalizing kisses on her upturned mouth.

"Your job? Why?" Her voice was weak, and she barely cared about his answer. Soon she would be lost in a swirl of sensation. "Do you have any clients up here?"

Their lips met in a long, lush kiss. "Only one," he answered shortly. "But as of today I'm no longer representing him." His face nuzzled into her bare shoulder as her hands caressed his back. "As a matter of fact, it was his portfolio I was immersed in this morning when the sun came up. You could say that we owe our meeting and this lovely moment to him."

"Oh?" she whispered dreamily. "Who is he?"

He kissed her neck and then her ears, letting the words slip out. "His name is T. K. Lester Akins."

Chapter Three

The name filtered quickly through Jenny's pleasured half-sense of reality, and hit her brain like a bolt of lightning. She sat up and stared at him, shocked.

"T. K. Lester Akins!"

"What's the matter?" he asked, taking her hands in his. "Surely that doesn't—"

"Are you crazy?" she demanded, pulling away from him.

"Why, no, I've never thought so," he said dryly. "I don't see why this should bother you. I already said I'm not representing Lester anymore, as of today."

"How very convenient!" she snapped. She looked down at her scantily clad body and shut her eyes for a moment in complete dismay. "What a mess. What a terrific mess. How did I get myself into this?" The rhetorical question was met with silence. Jenny reached for her clothes and began pulling them on hastily, buttoning her dress crookedly and squashing her shoes as she stepped on them.

Ryan watched her performance in astonishment, but when he spoke, it was with deliberate patience.

"Jenny," he began quietly. "Will you please listen to me?"

"Why should I?" she retorted indignantly, jerking hairpins haphazardly into her hair. "You could have told me sooner."

"Oh, is that all?" he asked mildly.

She stopped and faced him in total exasperation. "Is that all?" Her tone was incredulous. "Isn't that enough? I spent all that time telling you about Mr. Akins, and you never said a word. If you're his lawyer, then it was you who told him to turn down the offer from the commonwealth!"

He nodded complacently. "Yes. But that was before I knew the whole situation."

"So you're going to tell him you changed your mind?"

"No, I can't do that. Not if I'm not representing him anymore."

She let out a strangled cry of pure frustration. "Then what good is it going to do?"

"I'm sure Lester can be convinced," he said with a smug little smile. "But it won't be by me. I don't want to be involved with it from now on. For obvious reasons, I'd rather be involved with you."

"But I don't want to be involved with you!" she shouted, waving her arms for emphasis.

"You were pretty involved a few minutes ago," he pointed out calmly.

She smiled ironically. "Yes. But that was before I knew the whole situation." Grabbing her pocketbook, she marched to the door, her high heels clacking loudly on the wooden floor.

"You're making a mistake, Jenny," he said quietly.

She turned to look at him, and was startled for just a moment at the sight of him. He was sprawled across the bed, his smooth bare chest a golden brown in the dim light, his reddish hair tousled lazily across his forehead. But she gathered her resolve together. "I've already made the mistake," she answered just as quietly. "And you're it."

His roguish face broke into a smile, and his laughter was the last sound she heard as she slammed out the door.

Jenny was up and about before her alarm clock went off the next morning. She bustled around determinedly, avoiding all thoughts except those which centered around the vacation that was starting today. This time nothing was going to stop her from leaving on time and enjoying every second of her free time. She sipped a cup of black coffee hurriedly, letting the too-hot liquid scald her tongue as she consulted her road map. The early-morning rays of the sun left slanted stripes on the map, making her more conscious than ever of the time. She gulped down the last of the coffee and picked up the suitcase she had left sitting by the door.

Jenny lived in the top half of a farmhouse that was located at the edge of town. Her landlady, Mrs. Olsen, occupied the bottom half. As she clambered down the stairs with her suitcase in tow, she stopped to leave the hastily scribbled note she had prepared—"Leaving this morning. Be back next week. Please don't forget to take in my mail." As she was tucking the note into the box, she heard the distant sound of her telephone ringing upstairs.

She hesitated, then shook her head firmly and

marched outside to her car. Not this time, she told herself. This time you're going to get out of here without a hitch. She made it all the way to her car, when the front door of the house opened suddenly and Mrs. Olsen looked out.

"Oh, Jenny!" she called, her booming voice causing a nearby cow to low.

Jenny sighed in resignation. "Yes?" she called back.

"Margie is on my phone. She couldn't reach you upstairs, and she says it's urgent."

"But . . ." Mrs. Olsen disappeared inside the house, and Jenny dropped her suitcase with a bang. She ran into Mrs. Olsen's living room and picked up the phone. "Yes?" she said impatiently.

"Jen, it's me." Margie's voice sounded frantic. "I'm sorry to bother you, but this is really important."

"It better be," Jenny warned. "But first I want to know one thing. Will whatever you have to say stop me from going on this vacation?"

Margie hesitated. "Well . . . I don't know, Jenny. It's that guy from yesterday—Ryan Powers. I . . . well, I just think you ought to get over here, and fast."

"Oh, no you don't, Jenny said, refusing to be swayed. "First tell me what this is all about."

"Well," Margie hedged again. "He's . . . he's giving a tour."

"Good." Jenny laughed. "Let him. I told him yesterday we can use some tour guides. Be sure and tell him not to forget the silver collection in the west wing." This was met by a stunned silence. "Is that all?" she finished politely.

"Isn't that enough?" Margie squeaked. "Did you know he spent the night in the pioneer house?"

Damn, Jenny thought. I should have thought to kick him out before I left. But she responded coolly, "Yes. As a matter of fact, we . . . he ate dinner there." She deliberately pushed all thoughts of last night out of her mind, but it was no use. The pleasant recollection of his outlandish but undeniably appealing antics brought an unconscious smile to her face.

"He ate breakfast there, too," Margie informed her. "I had no idea. I mean, I practically walked in on him while he was taking a bath in the . . . Well, it was awfully embarrassing, that's all. And I wasn't the only one who barged in on him. I was giving a tour at the time. Twenty people walked into a house where a naked man was lathering himself in a tub. And do you know what he did?"

Jenny didn't know whether to laugh or explode. "No, what?"

"He welcomed us all and announced that he was the resident expert. Then, without batting an eye, he began giving a lecture on the history of the house. Sitting right there in the tub! I was shocked, though no one else seemed to mind at all. They just thought he was part of the museum staff. I managed to get them all out of there, but a few minutes later he emerged dressed in a minuteman uniform and took over my tour altogether. At this very moment, he's leading twenty visitors around the second floor of the museum. I really think you should come and speak to him."

Jenny hesitated, fascinated and annoyed at the same time. Margie heard the unspoken reluctance.

"Please, Jen," she pleaded. "It will only take a minute. I don't want to turn him in. You seemed to be able to talk to him."

"Oh, all right," Jenny relented. "But only for a minute. After that, I'm going on vacation, come hell or high water." She hung up the phone loudly and turned to see Mrs. Olsen standing in the archway.

"It's not serious, is it?" the buxom woman asked. "She hasn't locked herself in again, has she?"

"No, nothing like that. This time it's a wise guy who thinks he's Paul Revere." She marched out, leaving Mrs. Olsen to think what she liked.

Her car started without any trouble, and the chilly air cooled her ruffled temper as she drove off. It was amazing how one upstart of a man could cause so much trouble in such a short time. Not that he had actually harmed anything . . . and she had to admit there was a certain charm to his madness. As for last night . . . Well, it was fortunate she had found out about him when she did. The thought of a passionate scene with the infamous T. K. Lester Akins' lawyer almost made her blush. Only knowing that she had rejected him gave her the courage to face him again. He was the one who would have to make explanations, not her. It felt strange to realize that she had walked out on such a powerful man. She pictured him wheeling and dealing and manipulating everyone around him so that he got whatever he wanted. At last an overbearing New Yorker had gotten his comeuppance!

She realized that she was speeding, and slowed the car to an acceptable pace. Her thoughts about Ryan Powers had excited her more than by rights they should have, she thought. She forced herself to calm down at least to the car's pace, and by the time she pulled into the parking lot of the museum, she was ready for a confrontation.

Margie was waiting for her in the lobby. "Okay, Margie," Jenny said as she strode inside, "where is he? Let's get this over with."

"Second floor," Margie told her. "The weapons display."

"That sounds like a good place to do battle," Jenny quipped. They climbed the stairs to the upper level and hurried down the hall to the room that held the weapons. As they walked, they could hear Ryan's jovial voice booming as he discoursed on a point of history. Jenny paused for a moment outside the room to listen.

". . . and two of these dueling pistols were used in the famous Burr-Hamilton dispute. The argument was settled, of course, and everyone lived happily ever after . . . uh, except for Mr. Hamilton."

The sound of laughter floated down the hallway, but Jenny only frowned, puzzled. "The Hamilton-Burr duel?" she asked out loud. "I didn't know we had any dueling pistols at all."

"We don't," Margie explained in an anxious whisper. "That's the crazy thing about it. He's giving the tour, but his information is all wrong. Everything he's saying is incorrect."

Jenny's face was set grimly as she tiptoed to the entrance and surveyed the scene. A group of twenty people, many of them laden with cameras and small children, was gathered around the unmistakable figure of Ryan Powers. He was still clad in the minuteman uniform and she couldn't help but notice once again how very attractive and natural he looked in it. It was as if it had been tailor-made for him. Jenny winced as he reached inside the display case and lifted a long rifle.

"Now, this," he said confidently, "was made in Eli Whitney's factory. It was one of the first assembly-line guns, with the advantage that the parts were interchangeable. As a matter of fact, when the British attacked during the War of 1812—"

"Eli was still in diapers," Jenny called out. Everyone turned to look at her, and Ryan's face broke into a huge grin as she continued. "But then, if Mozart could write symphonies at the age of five, anything is possible." She walked into the room and stood in front of the group, deliberately ignoring Ryan.

He was not to be outdone, however. He bowed gallantly and said, "Good morning, Miss Moffatt. How kind of you to honor us with your presence."

"Thank you," she said icily. "Please, don't let me interrupt. I'd be fascinated to hear more."

He seemed slightly taken aback at being allowed to continue at all, but he gamely looked around for something else to talk about. Spying a long sword that was hooked onto the wall, he handed her the rifle and reached for the sword. When he turned to face her, he saw that she was holding the rifle in a firing position, much to the amusement of the crowd.

"Don't worry," she said. "It's not loaded." She added under her breath, "Unfortunately." She meant business, but he wasn't ready to quit, not yet.

Addressing the crowd authoritatively, he said,

"Now, this weapon was used during the Civil War under General Grant's—"

"Hey!" Jenny jumped back in alarm as the long sword brandished in front of her face. "Put that thing down!"

He lowered the sword obediently and waited to see what she would do. "You're off," she said, still eyeing the weapon.

"Off?"

"By a few wars. That sword never saw the Civil War."

"Oh. Spanish American?" he tried jovially.

"Nope. Up one more."

"World War One?" His smile was infectious. By now the tourists knew that something was amiss, but they didn't seem to mind at all. They were vastly entertained, and Jenny knew that she would have a hard time reprimanding him in front of them. She would look like a sour schoolmistress bawling out a mischievous bad boy. Ryan gently took the rifle from her and placed it back in the case. "Well, in any case," he said, "we won the war." He sounded a little doubtful, and he looked up to catch Jenny's disapproving but amused expression.

"You're right about one thing," she said.

"Oh?" He brightened. "What's that?"

"We did win that war. All of these weapons were used by American patriots on the various battlefields of our history."

"That's right," he confirmed judiciously, placing the sword back on its hooks. "And now, folks, if you'll follow me, I'll introduce you to the illustrious Akins family. Their portraits are in the next room."

She opened her mouth to protest, but the crowd

followed him immediately. She couldn't help but notice that the group was larger than usual. Ryan was like a magnet. Following curiously, she stood in back of the room and listened as he continued his impromptu narrative.

"William and Martha Akins," Ryan was saying without looking at the plaque under the portrait. His eyes looked up over the crowd and met hers where she stood quietly. Seeming to know that she wasn't going to challenge him, he went on more expansively. "This was painted in 1753."

Good memory, Jenny thought, surprised. She had shown him the portraits yesterday, and he wasn't looking at any of the furnished information. "William and Martha were the first Akinses to live in this mansion," he announced. Well, that was true, at least. His accuracy was improving. "William was the first manufacturer in Great Barrington. The old mill on Route 7 stands as a memorial to his hard work."

"That's right," Jenny said, half to herself. "But I never told you that."

Ryan heard her and smiled, moving on to the next portrait. "This is their son, Robert Randolph Akins. As you can see by his costume, he was involved in the Revolutionary War." The painting depicted a rather fierce-looking young man wearing an outfit that strangely resembled the one Ryan was wearing. The crowd pressed closer, examining the picture with interest, and Ryan moved in also, standing right next to it. A few cameras clicked as he continued the lecture, a slight twinkle stealing into his eyes. "Yes, Robert Randolph was an upstart, but he was also a great innovator. He was the one who was really responsible for establishing the town of Great Barrington, you know. He saved it from the hands of greedy colonial homesteaders who were intent on partitioning out huge tracts of land for commercial factory use. Those slimy devils were already making bids when our hero, Robert Randolph, purchased the entire area out from under them, including the land on which this museum stands." He stopped, stealing a glance at Jenny.

But she was only half-listening to his speech. Her mind was calculating swiftly as she realized why he had been so interested in the portraits yesterday. As the lawyer on the Akins case, she deduced, he had had to do his legal homework, researching the history that would allow Lester to develop this land. Ryan was still rattling cheerfully away, moving down the line of paintings until he stood next to the one of Geoffrey Akins, the turn-of-the-century financier who had once been the mayor of Great Barrington. Jenny watched him curiously, her eyes moving from his lively face to the painted face and then back again.

Suddenly she did a double-take, her eyes growing wide. Geoffrey Akins' definitive nose and shrewd eyes were mirrored in the face of Ryan Powers. There was a resemblance that could not be mistaken. Jenny looked back to the portrait of Robert Randolph Akins, dressed in his Revolutionary War outfit. This time her gaze was laced with shock.

Robert Randolph Akins was a dead ringer for Ryan Powers! For a moment she was thoroughly confused, thinking that she had truly gone back in time, or that Robert Randolph had somehow materialized, a time traveler from the twilight zone. She blinked, furiously trying to clear the image. But there was no doubt about it. Even the clothing was the same! Now that she thought about it, she remembered that the original version of the costume Ryan had appropriated had in fact once belonged to Robert Randolph. And now its copy was being worn by . . . one of his descendants! It had to be!

Her face flooded with enlightenment, something which was not lost on Ryan. His monologue continued effortlessly, but his clear blue eyes were pinned to hers, and she knew that he knew. She had discovered his secret.

"The spitting image," she whispered in wonder.

"What?" It was Margie, who had been standing behind her.

Jenny almost jumped. "Now I know why he showed such a keen interest in this room," she muttered. "It was his own family he was looking at."

"His family? Whose family?" Margie was quite baffled, but Jenny wasn't listening. She was staring hypnotically at Ryan as he finally wrapped up his tour.

"And that, ladies and gentlemen," he was saying, "is all. Please feel free to walk around the museum as long as you like, and don't forget to visit our souvenir shop."

Enthusiastic applause followed and then the crowd began to disperse. Ryan remained standing next to the portrait of Geoffrey Akins, and as Jenny looked at the two faces, she realized why she had thought she had seen him before. Now that it was so obvious, she wondered why she hadn't seen it sooner.

The room emptied slowly as people chatted among themselves about how much they had enjoyed the tour. Jenny had to admit to herself that his antics had been fascinating, misinformation and all. "I'll handle this," she said quietly to Margie, who took the hint and disappeared. She remained standing at the back of the room, staring at him with open challenge in her eyes.

"You shouldn't have run out on me last night," he said as the last of the visitors filed out. "You never gave me a chance to explain."

"Explain what, Mr. Ryan Powers Akins?" she huffed, ready for a fight. "That you lied to me?"

He almost missed a beat. "My name is Powers, though I admit my father was an Akins," he said. "And I didn't lie to you. That's not fair."

She walked forward to confront him, determined not to succumb as she had last night. "Of course you did. You never told me who you were. You let me go on about the insensitive fools who were going to destroy the Berkshires. Why didn't you say something?"

"You have very sharp eyes," he said, grimacing. "I must say I'm impressed. As for last night, I was enjoying myself far too much to spoil things. We were getting along so well."

His smile was just a little too confident, she thought. He relaxed his stance and strolled forward to stand over her, looking down into her eyes. Once again she found herself fascinated by the way his face seemed to change constantly, always underlining his words, but never revealing his thoughts. His hands found her arms suddenly, and she shivered involuntarily at his touch. "I hate unfinished business," he went on in a low voice. Now she was thoroughly confused. Did he mean the land business? Or what had happened between them last night? She started to back away, but he followed her, and she stopped abruptly. She couldn't let him back her right into the wall.

"That's better," he said in the same low, silky voice. "You should never run out on a man until you know exactly what his intentions are."

"And what are yours?"

"I intend to make love to you by the end of the day."

"Is that so?" It was impossible to remain cool after a statement like that, but Jenny tried anyway. "And what makes you think I'm interested?"

"Oh, I already know you're interested. As interested as I am. I just want to be sure that you don't misunderstand me. I'm not an ogre, you know."

"I never said you were," she said slowly.

They were interrupted by a group of schoolchildren shepherded by a teacher, and their conversation was halted. The children milled noisily around the room, some of them staring curiously at Ryan's costume.

"Let's get out of here," he suggested, and she found herself nodding in agreement. Despite her impatience and her strong desire to begin her vacation, she sorely wanted to get to the bottom of all this.

"Come with me," she said, leading him outside.

"Where are you taking me?"

"You'll see," she said firmly. "To a very appropriate place. She took him behind the museum and walked right up to the pioneer house.

"Now," she said, taking control, "I want you out of those clothes immediately. "And—"

"I knew you'd see it my way," he said brightly. "I told you I'd be making love to you by the end of the day. I never dreamed it would happen so soon."

Jenny refused to be nettled. "You know what I mean. You can change inside and leave those clothes where you found them."

"Yes, ma'am," he answered, military style. "Anything else?"

"Yes," she replied coolly. "When you're finished, you can tell me how you happen to be mixed up in all of this. As an Akins, you must have more to do with it than I realized."

His eyes twinkled. "Well, you're right about that. But let's take this one thing at a time. Right now I could use a little help getting out of these breeches. As you recall, the lacings are rather tricky."

She hesitated, but relented when she remembered that the lacings were around the back. "Oh, all right. Come inside for a minute. I don't want the immediate world to see me undressing you."

They entered the small house, which still smelled pleasantly of last night's dinner. She was glad to see that everything had been cleaned, tidied, and restored to its original state. Nonetheless the lingering aroma teased Jenny's senses, reminding her of the scene she had vowed to forget. Ryan turned his broad back to her obediently, and she struggled with the lacings, which had somehow become knotted.

"I can't quite . . . Oh!" she exclaimed, as one of

the strings broke in her impatient hand. "Now look what I've done!"

He put his hands on his narrow hips and shifted his weight, flexing the muscles in his back at the same time. "Don't worry about it," he said calmly. "It can be fixed." Before she knew what was happening, he turned around and eased the loosely fitted shirt from his body, leaving his bronzed chest bare. "You can stay if you like," he went on just as calmly. "I promise not to ravish you—yet."

"That's quite all right," she said rather weakly, mesmerized by the sight of his lean, powerful body. "I think I'll make a fast exit right about now."

"But what about all those fascinating explanations you wanted to hear?"

"Later," she said firmly, heading for the door.

"Maybe I'll leave the explanations to Lester," he mused. "After all, the inheritance is only half mine. Whatever he does with his half from now on is his business."

Jenny froze, her hand on the door.

"Staying after all?" he asked. "Then you'd better lock that door. I wouldn't want some unsuspecting tourist to pop in while I'm changing."

She didn't move. "Your half?" she repeated in a daze. "Of the inheritance? Of course! You're the other grandson! Why didn't I realize?"

"I suppose because you were too busy being self-righteous and angry with me," he answered smugly. He walked forward with a distinct swagger, leaning casually against the door so that she couldn't leave. "But as I told you before, I'm no longer involved with Lester at all. The guy's a bum, believe me. I'd much rather be involved with you."

Jenny found her voice and looked up at him incredulously. "But why did you tell him to turn down our offer?"

He shrugged. "I didn't know anything about it then, except that there was more money in developing than in taking your offer. I'm a businessman. I make deals all the time. This was just one more to be weighed like all the others. The terms weren't quite right, so I said no. But of course, that was all before I came here and met you. And before I retired."

"And now you've changed your mind?" She eyed him suspiciously. "It's that easy?"

His bright blue eyes looked straight into hers, free of guile. "Yes," he said simply. "I don't want to represent Lester anymore. He can do what he likes. But he'll have to fight me if he wants to horn in on this territory. I've decided to live here, you know. I don't want this area torn up any more than you do." He smiled, a disarmingly charming smile that went straight to her heart. "I'm your neighbor now. I'm on your side, not his."

"Oh, Ryan," she whispered. "Why didn't you tell me all this last night?"

"You hardly gave me a chance. And I'm not in the habit of divulging more information than necessary. It's an old business precaution of mine. I had no idea you'd be so touchy about it."

"But surely you could have said something."

"Not before I had all the facts. First I like to see which way the wind is blowing. Then I decide what course to take. I went through a serious change yesterday, you know. A change that led to my retirement."

She studied him, her eyes searching his face. "You're really serious about that, aren't you?"

"Of course I'm serious." There was no humor on his face at all. "Don't you believe me?"

"No," she said after a moment, a slow smile spreading across her face. "But we'll let that take care of itself. Personally, I don't think you could sit still for more than a day. You'd go crazy up here with nothing to do, especially in the winter."

He said nothing, but he continued to gaze at her, looking down with frank longing softening the lines of his face. A silent moment passed between them, one in which time seemed to stop for a breathless drop of eternity, and then his lips were on hers, drinking in the taste of her as he pressed her slender frame to his bare, smoothly muscled chest. Her senses became flooded with the feel of him, and she forgot everything except the sudden lightning need to lose herself with him.

Their tongues met in a feverish duet, sending fresh waves of desire coursing through their bodies. The kissing stopped for only a split second before it began again, just as fierce, just as intense. Jenny's eyes were still closed as he pulled himself away from her, leading her quickly to the bed.

"Wait a minute, Ryan," she gasped. "Someone could walk in and—"

"Don't worry," he answered shortly. "I took your advice and locked the door. We're safe."

"But—"

Her objection was drowned in the new assault that obliterated reality. He rained kisses over her face and her neck and left slow, teasing circles with his tongue until she was limp with pleasure. Her hands reached out blindly and found his bare chest, relishing the smooth, hard feel of him and the quickened movements from his rapid breathing. He groaned suddenly, igniting her even further, and she fell back as his hands found their way down her body. In a moment, her pale blue sweater was pushed up and over her head. Her breasts trembled inside their thin covering of white lace, which was quickly pushed aside under his demanding fingers. His hands cupped her small breasts tenderly at first, exploring their firm sweetness, but then his touch became feverish as he savored her lush femininity. Jenny watched him with half-veiled eyes, her hands lost in the shock of reddish-brown hair that just grazed her chest.

"You are so beautiful," he whispered, and she believed him, feeling more womanly and desirable than she ever had before, because he saw her that way.

It was a moment to savor, to cherish, but it was not to be fully realized. A sudden knock on the door jerked them both back to earth, Jenny instinctively covering her breasts with her arms.

"Yes?" she called out weakly.

"Jenny? Are you in there? It's me, Margie!"

The door rattled insistently, and Jenny struggled to sit up, hastily refastening her bra and pulling her sweater over her head. "Just a second, Margie. I'll be right there."

Ryan watched her coolly, but the remains of the interrupted passion were still etched on his features. "I have a feeling I know what's going to happen next," he said in a low voice.

"You do seem to know everything," Jenny said

rather grumpily. "You're full of surprises, I'll grant you that."

"Jenny?" Margie called. "Are you all right? Who are you talking to?"

"Shall I hide in the closet?" Ryan asked with an obliging grin.

"Don't be ridiculous. There is no closet," she hissed back. "Coming, Margie!" she called in a louder voice.

"You won't believe who's here," Margie shouted back conversationally. "It's him."

Jenny stopped in her tracks. "Who?"

"Him. T. K. Lester Akins in person. He just got in from Houston. And he's not alone. A whole bunch of land developers are here with him." Margie sounded breathlessly eager to impart this startling bit of news.

"My, that was fast," Ryan commented, lounging back on the bed. "He must have taken the red-eye flight. He certainly is eager."

Jenny wheeled. "You know about this? What did you do, send him an engraved invitation?"

"Jenny!" Margie's voice was commanding. "Open that door!"

Jenny marched to the door and swung it open impatiently, letting Margie in. Margie entered with unbridled curiosity, her eyes stopping dead when they focused on the intriguing figure of Ryan. "Oh . . ." she said, flustered despite the merry glint in her eyes. "I didn't realize. Am I interrupting anything?"

"No," Jenny said firmly, just as Ryan nodded emphatically.

"Well, uh . . . I could come back, I guess. But . . .

you see, these men are all inside waiting to see you." This was followed by a sudden giggle that was met with complete silence.

"They want to see whom?" Jenny asked, trying to sound logical. "Me? Or him?" She pointed at Ryan, who merely grinned.

Margie hesitated. "Uh . . . both of you, I guess."

"I'm supposed to be on vacation," Jenny said to the room. "And today is Saturday." She turned to Ryan. "This is your fault."

"Fault? I wouldn't put it quite that way," Ryan commented dryly. "I thought we could sit down and straighten things out before they got out of hand. This is the perfect opportunity."

"Oh. But why wasn't I informed? Who else is going to be at this little meeting?"

"No one special. Just the mayor, a representative from the governor's office, someone from the local Chamber of Commerce . . . and, of course, you."

"I see. How convenient." Jenny tried to frown, but then she sighed. "I suppose I'd better get going if I'm ever going to make it out of here today. Lester just showed up, did he? I guess the knack of making dramatic entrances runs in your family."

Ryan looked a bit disgruntled, and he waved an arm. "Go on ahead. I'll be there shortly."

"I thought you were no longer Lester's lawyer."

"I'm not," he said. "But I am the other inheritor."

"That's true." Jenny sighed. "Well, don't be too long. We don't have all day."

She and Margie left the house as Ryan reached for the business suit that he had hung up to dry the night before. They walked up the path to the museum, Jenny reflecting irritably on what a magnificent day it was to go on a vacation.

"He doesn't seem too anxious to see his cousin," Margie said after a pause.

"Who? Oh, you mean Ryan. I thought you meant Lester."

"Lester too. I gather they don't get along very well."

Jenny thought for a moment. "No, I don't think they do. Ryan said that Lester's a bum. I wonder why he agreed to act as Lester's lawyer? It's too bad for cousins to feel that way about each other."

"I agree," Margie said. "And they're both very strong-willed." There was another pause, and their feet crunched the gravel. "But totally different. As different as night and day."

Chapter Four

"Mr. T. K. Lester Akins, I'd like you to meet Ms. Jennifer Moffatt," Margie said with a slight flourish.

Jenny couldn't help staring as a large, brawny man wearing a western suit and a cowboy hat eased himself up from a chair, extending his hand.

"Howdy, ma'am," he said congenially. He looked completely outlandish in the colonial meeting room with its high, arched windows and austere wooden furniture. Next to the framed portraits of New England dignitaries, he appeared to be not only an anachronism, but out of his geographical context as well.

"How do you do?" she said politely, finding her voice. "I . . . you'll have to excuse my informal appearance. I didn't know about this meeting until just a few minutes ago."

Lester's laughter boomed through the room. "Why, that's all right, little lady. Out where I come from, you'd do just fine." He shook her hand heartily, his tanned face glowing with good spirit. It was impossible not to smile back at him. Jenny noticed that his eyes were just as blue as Ryan's and that they carried the same shrewd awareness. "I'm glad you called this meeting," he went on enthusiastically. "It's a good—"

"*I* called this meeting?" Jenny repeated. "I'm afraid you've got it wrong."

"No," he said staunchly, shaking his head. "My lawyer called and said you wanted us all here, on the double. I was happy to oblige, because I want to get on with our little building project. I'm glad we were finally able to see eye to eye about that."

"I really don't know what is going on here," Jenny said, "but there isn't going to be any building going on around here." She wanted to add that Ryan had obviously either lied or had something up his sleeve, but she kept herself in check. He would have a chance to explain himself very soon.

A layer of Lester's expansive charm fell away. "I'm sure you must be mistaken," he said smoothly. "My lawyer said—"

"I've met your lawyer," she cut in. "And you can stop playing Mr. Nice Guy. Our answer is still no." She didn't add that Ryan was now on her side and that Lester didn't have a prayer without his cousin's support. Ryan could inform Lester of that himself.

"Are we back to that again?" Lester sighed and sat down abruptly. "I thought Ryan had agreed to everything. He's a good businessman, I'll admit that. He sure knows how to go where the money is. In this case, he agreed to let me handle the plans for the whole plot of land, the part he inherited as well as my half. He was just going to wrap up the financial and legal details." He shook his head, genuinely unconvinced. "No, you can't chase that old son of a gun away, not when this kind of profit is involved."

"The profit here," Jenny said proudly, "is aesthetic rather than monetary." She refused to believe that Ryan would be swayed by profit now that he had seen the beauty of his legacy.

"Now, don't be such a hoity-toity," Lester said, propping his right foot on his left knee. It was such a funny expression, and he said it with such a friendly air, that Margie, who had remained quiet, her large brown eyes moving between the two adversaries like a spectator at a tennis match, broke into gentle laughter.

Jenny laughed too, breaking the tension, and Lester sat back, smiling triumphantly. "All right," she began again. "I'm not really so high and mighty. But I really don't understand your attitude. After all, this house was your grandfather's. Your ancestors go back over two hundred years in this town. Doesn't that mean anything to you?"

It was a simple enough question, but Lester frowned thoughtfully, eyeing her carefully before answering. "What exactly did Ryan tell you?" he asked.

"Tell me? About what?" she hedged.

He paused again, clearly not wishing to reveal what was on his mind. "Why don't we just stick to the agenda?" he suggested finally. "I took a very early flight out here to work out any details the developers might have with heavy equipment and so forth. We don't want to interfere with traffic or local business. We just want to do a good job."

Jenny almost blanched at the mention of building equipment. This man obviously meant business, and she would have to do something about it, fast. "But I thought we were going to discuss the latest offer from the commonwealth of Massachusetts," she wailed. "You can't just show up here and start taking over. And furthermore, I think you'll find that Ryan has had second thoughts."

"I doubt that," Lester sniffed. "Ryan would love to see this house leveled and the land divided up into tiny pieces. He can't do anything about the house, because old man Josiah left it to the town. Not that he cares two bits about this house, like I said. But as for the land, well, he and I just might see eye to eye about that."

Jenny faced him squarely. "And if he changes his mind?"

"It wouldn't matter much to me." He shrugged. "I'll just go ahead with my half like I planned. I've got all the good land, the acreage with the view. Ryan only got the parts in the valley."

She was thoroughly confused by now, but she didn't want him to know that. She looked at Margie for a clue, but Margie's eyes were pinned on Lester, and there was a sparkle in them that hadn't been there before. Turning back to Lester, she tried another angle. "And what if Ryan does want to develop?" she asked, repressing a shudder. "Supposing his plans don't coincide with yours?"

"That's what I'm trying to tell you, little lady, but you don't want to listen. Ryan will go where the money is, no doubt about that. We're here to figure all that out. That's what this meeting is supposed to be about."

Jenny could think of nothing to say. She had been sure that Ryan was sincere, but he hadn't told her everything. And she had almost lost herself in his embrace only a few scant minutes ago. This thought, coupled with the memory of last night's short-lived scene, almost made her groan with dismay. She couldn't keep sticking up for a man just because he was devilishly attractive. By now her confusion was written clearly on her face, and Lester sat back serenely, confident of his position.

Jenny was vastly relieved to see the door open at that moment, but it wasn't Ryan who was entering the room. Four men attired in business suits came in, followed by the mayor of the town, who was more casually dressed in gray slacks and a sweater. Jenny greeted the mayor and introduced him to Lester, and the four men identified themselves as Fred Vogel and his son Frank, partners in a land-development corporation, the representative from the governor's office, and the representative from the Chamber of Commerce. The group shook hands all around and took seats at the oblong conference table. They all looked expectantly at Jenny, and she realized that they were counting on her, as head of the museum, to chair the meeting. I barely know what's going on, she thought, wishing frantically that Ryan would appear to clear things up.

"I'm very glad to see all of you here," she began carefully, "but I'm afraid that we'll have to sort out some facts before continuing."

"We've already sorted things out," Lester broke in impatiently. "Let's get to the heart of the issue."

"But that is the essence of the problem," Jenny countered smoothly. "We don't know what the heart of the issue is."

Lester looked around hastily. "Where's Ryan, anyway?" he asked. "We can't discuss this without him."

"That's very true. I'm sure he'll be here at any moment." She turned to the mayor and the other men. "Apparently the two Akinses do not agree on what should be done with their inheritance."

"Well, that's nothing new," the mayor said tiredly.

Fred Vogel looked up, suddenly alarmed. "What do you mean? I thought we were here to talk about the condominium project. Mr. Akins here is all set to go."

"Yes, but . . ." Jenny stopped and sighed. This whole situation was tied up in knots, and it was all Ryan's fault. Was he working with his cousin, or against him?

"We don't want to see this deal fall through, Miss Moffatt," Frank Vogel said. "This is a big contract for us, you know. We aren't going to bow out gracefully."

"Well, we aren't going to tolerate an invasion," Margie said unexpectedly.

"Then you'll have to call in the Army to keep us out," Frank quipped.

"That's an excellent idea!" Ryan's voice echoed through the room, and Jenny stifled a groan. Everyone turned to look at him, Margie covering her mouth with her hand to hide her smile.

Ryan was still attired in his minuteman uniform, and a sword hung threateningly from his hand. His arrival was met with various shades of disapproval and disbelief, broken by Lester's sudden snicker.

"Well, Ryan," he said condescendingly. "Still insisting on being the center of attention, eh? I can see you haven't changed."

"I thought you were going to get out of that uniform," Jenny said tactfully, trying to sound as if everything were normal.

Ryan grinned, his eyes dancing over them. "My suit is still damp. You wouldn't want me to catch cold, would you?"

He strolled into the room, and Jenny watched him the way she would watch a bomb that was about to go off. She knew that his outward facade had little to do with the energy and power that was inside.

"Nice to see you, Lester," he said evenly. "You're looking well."

"And you're looking mighty interesting in that getup," Lester returned.

"This getup," Ryan explained, "is a copy of clothes that belonged to our ancestor. You really should pay a visit to the portrait room, Lester. It could change you."

"Well, it certainly changed you. What kind of switcheroo are you trying to pull?" Lester's tone was barely civil, and Jenny hastened to intervene.

"Uh . . . why don't you sit down, Mr. Akins? I'm sure we'd all like to get started."

"That suits me just fine," said Lester. "I'd like everyone here to know right off the bat that I'm not a villain in this situation." He stopped, turning deliberately to Ryan. "As a matter of fact, I'm planning on moving here myself. So you all can hardly accuse me of trying to spoil the area."

"You?" Ryan's voice was now openly hostile, and Jenny recoiled in surprise. "Don't be ridiculous. I can stop you anytime I want. Our grandfather's will isn't as open-and-shut as you think."

Ryan's menacing self-assurance gave Lester pause for only a moment. "You're bluffing," he announced flatly. "You're just up to your old tricks."

"Am I?" Ryan smiled coolly. "We'll just see about that."

"You can't stop me from doing anything," Lester insisted. "Just go ahead and try." The two men looked at each other truculently, each unwilling to back down, like two schoolboys daring each other to cry uncle. For a minute, no one said a word. Then Jenny tried again.

"It seems that both of you are planning to move here. That's very interesting, because—"

She got no further. Lester let out a whoop of surprise. "Him? He's planning on moving *here*? If that don't beat all! He's got something up his sleeve, all right, but I sure don't know what it is."

"I would very much like to know what all this is about," the mayor said sternly. "I wish someone would enlighten me."

"It's very simple," Ryan answered him, to Jenny's vast relief. "My client wants to develop the land here. I don't. However, he's no longer my client as of today. What he fails to understand is that all this can be worked out amicably. But his attitude is so belligerent that I'm afraid we'll all have to exercise a considerable amount of patience."

Lester's face grew redder and redder during this speech, and he jumped out of his chair, banging his fist on the table. "Hang it all, Ryan, I just wish you'd make up your mind! What do you mean, you don't want to develop? Why'd you make me come all the way out here for?"

Ryan's cool smile was infuriating. "I told you. To straighten things out." Lester glared at him, completely baffled.

The mayor threw his pen on the table and stood up. "If anything is going to get straightened out," he said wearily, "I hope you'll let me know. But this meeting does not seem to be making any headway, and I have other things to do." He glanced at the two developers. "I'm afraid you gentlemen are just going to have to wait."

Ryan also stood up, his demeanor suddenly all business, despite the eighteenth-century costume. "I'd like to make a concrete suggestion," he said.

The mayor looked at him pointedly. "I wish you would."

"Now that Mr. Akins is here, perhaps he'd like to stay and evaluate the situation." He paused, flashing Lester an icy smile. "Perhaps he can be convinced to change his mind."

"Well, you're not going to change it today, that's for sure," Lester huffed.

"Good," Ryan said. "Then this meeting can safely be adjourned. We'll all meet again at a more appropriate time." He spoke with such authority that the other men got up politely and began to leave. Jenny suspected that they were more than glad to be temporarily rid of this problem, realizing that the two inheritors would have to settle things between themselves.

When only she, Margie, Lester, and Ryan were left in the room, there was a sudden quiet, as if the aborted meeting had never taken place.

"Well, that settles that." Ryan chuckled to himself.

"That settles nothing, and you know it." Lester chortled. "You'll be hearing from me, Ryan. Make no doubt about that."

"Fine," Ryan said mildly, waving him off as if he were a mosquito. "But in the meantime, enjoy Great Barrington. You just might surprise yourself."

"I'll just do that," Lester answered stonily. "I'm in no rush. Now, how do I get out of here?"

"I'll show you out," Margie volunteered.

"That's very kind of you, little lady. Most kind indeed." Lester gallantly offered his arm to Margie, who took it promptly and led him out.

Jenny turned to Ryan, a slight frown on her face. He said nothing, watching her with a shadow of a grin.

"What just happened here?" she asked slowly. "Why do I have the feeling that we've all just been had?"

"All of us except me, you mean." She nodded. "You're wrong," he continued, shaking his head. "Me too. All of us were sold out years ago."

Her eyes narrowed. "What's that supposed to mean?"

Ryan didn't answer her. He walked over to the window and gazed out raptly. Then he turned suddenly and faced her. "Well," he said, "where do we go from here?"

Jenny hesitated. "We?"

"You and me. We were rudely interrupted back in the pioneer house. What shall we do now?"

"Do?"

"You certainly are full of words." He walked forward, towering over her in his costume, and her eyes fell.

"Ryan . . ." She faltered. "If you recall, I was about to go on vacation."

"I know. But something came up. Me. And I got carried away."

"I didn't." She knew her statement wasn't true. He *had* swept her off her feet. But she didn't like the way he tried to put words in her mouth. "What about my long-awaited vacation?"

"We'll go together," he answered promptly. "I just have to stop off and get some clothes, and we'll—"

"No!" She felt obliged to discourage his impulsive idea, even though a part of her suddenly blossomed at the suggestion.

"No?" His eyes studied her. "What are you running away from?"

"You," she said directly. "It's . . . it's too soon. We just met and I don't think I'm ready to run off with you for a whole week." Her hands gestured vaguely. "What if we can't stand each other after a day or two?"

"That won't happen and you know it."

She felt herself slipping. The idea of a madcap spree with him was certainly tempting. No! No, it was crazy. She shook her head in a firm negative.

"Can't I convince you?" he pressed.

"No, you can't. I'm not that gullible. I've made up my mind."

He responded by once again drawing her to him, his hand sensuously burrowing into the hair at the back of her head as he brought her lips to his, and she did nothing to stop him. The memory of how easily he had aroused her was all too fresh, and she couldn't resist the sweetness with which he fired her passion. She felt the glow rise inside of her, letting it linger as the kiss ended. She tried to avoid looking at him, but he lifted her chin and stared into her eyes.

"Now what do you say?" he whispered hoarsely. "Have I convinced you?"

"No," she said, hoping to halt his advance, even though her cheeks were flushed and her voice was shaky.

He only smiled and kissed her again, this time enfolding her in strong, sure arms as his tongue easily found its way to hers. The second kiss was like a magical conversation, so sweetly intimate that the familiar flames rose swiftly, leaving her utterly helpless in his grasp, longing for more.

Her eyes fluttered open only to meet his questioning gaze. After a long moment she shook her head and pulled away from him, though she had to fight to find the strength of will. She didn't like being pressured, no matter how convincing he was. Giving him no chance to pursue her, she headed to the door, trying to ignore her own inner trembling.

"I'll be back in a week," she said, forcing her voice to be steady. "And then we'll have plenty of time to—"

"No, Jenny. You're wrong." He was at her side in a second, determination shining in his blue eyes. The look that passed between them carried emotions too intense for words, and he made sure she felt its power before enveloping her in an embrace that made her tingle with anticipation. She could feel the strong, fluid lines of his body demanding, needing her response, she could smell the piny scent that emanated from him, and she tasted a dreamy hint of sweet cinnamon that seemed transported from a secret world.

Somehow she managed to gather the shreds of her willpower to whisper brokenly, "Ryan, I don't think—"

"Good," he muttered. "Don't think. Just feel."

He lowered his face to hers once more, but even as she prepared for the swept-away feeling, he surprised her completely by maintaining a gentleness that flooded her with longing. His sudden restraint was what did it. Dimly she realized that he was not pushing her; he was pleading with her to recognize the yearning that so desperately needed to be satisfied, the yearning that was his as well as hers.

Jenny's eyes opened slowly. "Your car or mine?" she asked.

Mercifully, his smile was not triumphant.

A few minutes later, she was sitting next to him, letting the comfortable silence between them smooth the way. Her suitcase had been tossed into the backseat, and the car glided peacefully along Route 123. Jenny felt delightfully carefree, ready and willing to let the coming week bring what it might.

But as they approached the parkway, she saw that he was heading onto the southern entrance ramp instead of going north to the turnpike.

"Hey!" she said, sitting up in alarm. "You took the wrong turn."

"No, I didn't," he answered. "I told you—I've got to stop and get some clothes."

She stared at him for a moment, utterly confused, and then at the highway markers, which were passing rapidly by the side of the road. The realization hit her in a rush. "Oh, no! Your clothes?" She turned around in the bucket seat to face him. "Are they where I think they are?"

"Of course." He smirked. "Where else? We're going to New York City."

Chapter Five

The two-and-a-half-hour drive down the parkway was a peaceful one that took them through gentle hills and rolling farmland. Spring always came late to the Berkshires, but the farther south they drove, the more green were the trees. It was as though they were watching the seasons change before their eyes, as fat buds were replaced by tiny rolls, and then by full-blown leaves. Jenny remained quiet, taking in the view and accepting the unexpected detour as a kind of fateful adventure.

But the moment they crossed into Manhattan, as if a magic wand had passed over them, everything changed. The road, full of potholes, bounced the car wildly. The traffic became heavier, and Jenny could feel the pace of the city as surely as if a dose of adrenaline had been injected into her blood. Ryan drove expertly, with a rather predatory air, and Jenny's eyes darted everywhere, trying to see everything at once. To their left was the thin strip of Riverside Park, filled with winding paths and sturdy citified trees. To their right was the Hudson River, dividing New York from New Jersey, little more than a stone's throw away.

The many inhabitants of the park were all

occupied—walking, bicycling, jogging, playing Frisbee and volleyball, and picnicking on the grass. This one park appeared to hold as many people as the entire town of Great Barrington, and there was something exhilarating and incredible about the variety and activity.

"Look at all those people!" Jenny exclaimed.

"It's Saturday," he answered gruffly. "It's a nice day, and everyone has to get out and release energy. This city does that to you. If you don't alleviate the pressure, you go crazy."

"Really? And what did you do to alleviate the pressure?"

He laughed sharply. "I quit, that's what I did. But before that, I spent time lifting weights at a health club."

Jenny wasn't impressed. "Sounds dull."

"It's not supposed to be fascinating."

"But look at everyone here! Look at that old couple over there, on roller skates. You could have done something like that, instead of going to a boring old health club."

"Lots of people here go to health clubs. There's nothing wrong with it." He swerved suddenly to avoid a cab that was barreling down from the next lane.

"Yes, but it's so isolating," she persisted. "Did you ever go to this park?"

He had to think about it for a moment. "No, I guess not. So what?"

She was astonished. "You've lived here all this time and you never went to this park?"

"No," he repeated, annoyed. "Don't make such a

big deal out of it. So I never went to Riverside Park. So what?"

"Okay, okay," she said, backing off. "Sorry I mentioned it. I just thought it was odd, that's all."

Ryan took an exit, and suddenly they were in the heart of the city. Tall, seemingly endless buildings surrounded them. The people on the sidewalks looked like ants in comparison. Jenny craned her neck to look up, and Ryan chuckled.

"Don't look up," he said dryly. "It's better if you don't. You don't want to know how small you are. Just look straight ahead."

Jenny did, and saw the mouth of a subway entrance. The screech of an arriving train came from under the street, and a minute later a horde of people spilled out, scurrying at once in different directions. "It's like a painting in constant motion," she murmured, her eyes glowing. Ryan glanced at her sharply but said nothing.

He drove across town, cutting through the graceful landscapes of Central Park, and Jenny looked everywhere, trying to take it all in. "This park is beautiful!" she cried. "I had no idea! Look at that little house over there—oh, it says they have puppet shows. Isn't that delightful? I always thought Central Park was a good place to get mugged."

"It is," he assured her sourly. "In the middle of the night." They pulled up in front of a large building on Fifth Avenue, where a uniformed doorman hurried to help them out.

"Home from the war, Mr. Powers?" he asked.

Ryan looked down at his minuteman outfit and laughed. "In a way. We won't be needing the car until tomorrow." He took Jenny's arm and ushered her into the lobby.

"What do you mean, tomorrow?" she bristled. "We were only supposed to get some clothes and then be on our way!"

"I told you, Jennifer," he whispered into her ear as they waited for the elevator to arrive, "I intend to make love to you by the end of the day. I'm not taking any chances."

Her mouth fell open in surprise, but she stifled her reaction as the elevator doors opened and a group of people came out. They waited until the elevator was empty before stepping inside. Ryan pushed the top button marked PH.

"What's a PH?" she asked.

"Penthouse."

"Oh. Now, what's going on here? I thought we were just stopping to—"

"I told you. I intend to make love to you before the day is out, and I'm starting right now." He drew her into his arms and sought her mouth with his, using his tongue to part her lips and invade the warmth his passion had created. The elevator rose gracefully.

"Ryan!" she gasped, pulling away. "What are you doing?"

"I told you. I intend—"

"I know, I know. But *here*?"

"It's as good a place as any to start." Once again she was swept into his arms, but the elevator stopped at the second floor and the doors opened, revealing a workman with a bucket in his hand. He stared at the affectionate couple but did nothing, letting the doors close without getting on.

"This isn't fair," Jenny announced. "You can't trick me into staying here." With that, she bounced over to the panel on the wall and punched every one of the buttons.

"What the hell did you do that for?" he asked in amazement. "Now it will take forever for us to get up there!"

"I know," she answered smugly. "Which will give us the time we need to discuss the situation."

"There's nothing to discuss," he said angrily, sweeping her back into his arms. His mouth came down on hers, overwhelming her with masculine energy. She closed her eyes for only a split second, but her traitorous body responded in spite of her resolve, and she felt the sweet, familiar arousal creeping up like a budding vine. The elevator came to a halt at the third floor and they broke apart, waiting patiently for the doors to open and close again. As soon as they did, Jenny and Ryan flung themselves at each other, continuing the ardent kiss as if they had all the time in the world. But the fourth floor intruded on their private world, and once again they were forced to wait until they were alone.

"This is ridiculous," Jenny gasped between kisses.

"It was your idea," he reminded her, too filled with desire to argue. By the fifth floor, his hands had found their way under her sweater and were playing delicately with the sensitive peaks of her breasts. When they stopped, she managed a devilish smile, and he laughed brokenly. As soon as the doors closed, they lunged at each other, their hands roaming hungrily with blind need.

By the time they arrived at the tenth floor, they didn't know how they would even survive the exquisite anticipation. The elevator continued to lurch upward, floor by floor, and Jenny was beginning to care less and less who saw them. But at the sixteenth floor, an elderly couple got on and stood in front of them. Jenny restrained herself and stood helplessly, holding tightly to Ryan's hand. The woman pushed the button for the twenty-fourth floor, and for the next eight floors the doors opened and closed systematically as the four of them stood there. The elderly couple apparently didn't notice anything amiss, but as they passed the twentieth floor, Jenny felt Ryan's hand slowly sneaking under her sweater. He caught her nipple between two fingers, toying with it gently but firmly, and Jenny closed her eyes against the uprush of feeling that threatened to overtake her. The elderly couple remained motionless, but Jenny thought the whole world must know what was going on in this elevator. She was almost relieved when Ryan's hand left her breast and slipped down her torso, but before she could stop him, his hand slid into the waistband of her jeans. Jenny stifled the cry that would have escaped her, standing frozen while his hand moved lower, gently tugging at the hidden curls that concealed the place he sought. His feathery touches were accomplished in silence and the glint in his eye was mutely radiant, but the response in Jenny's loins was like a siren. She didn't know how her knees were still supporting her. The woman in front of them shifted casually, turning her head for a moment so that she caught sight of Ryan in her peripheral vision. He never missed a beat, giving her a cool, polite smile before she turned back to face front again. Jenny didn't believe the torment would ever end.

The elevator doors seemed to open in slow motion at the twenty-fourth floor, and the old couple stirred themselves. They exited slowly, and the woman stumbled slightly at the threshold, so that the man caught her arm to help her. Then he hit the doors with his arm as they were closing so that they mechanically opened again, giving the couple time to leave safely. They both ambled down the hall as the doors finally closed again, coming together slowly with a bang. Jenny threw her arms around Ryan, kissing him feverishly, their tongues meeting in a lush duet. His strong arms crushed her close, and her whole body was alive, singing with passion and anticipation.

She couldn't bear to tear herself away from him at the twenty-fifth floor. Their mouths parted, but they still clung to each other, Jenny's arms around his neck. "Oh, Ryan," she murmured, "what if someone sees us?"

"I don't care," he answered savagely. "I want you."

He kissed her again, slowly, as if to savor the delicious sensation, closing his eyes in rapture, and the elevator continued its slow, dispassionate journey. There was no one at the twenty-sixth floor, but Jenny and Ryan didn't notice. They were too busy exploring each other, lost in their own private world. Each stop only added to their excitement, bringing them closer and closer to the end of the endless ride.

But at the thirty-eighth floor, the sound of voices

intruded. They looked up breathlessly to see a young couple waiting to board the elevator, and Jenny's only thought was that she was annoyed at the interruption. "Sorry," Ryan said with a ragged smile, "this car's taken." The doors closed on the astonished faces of the young couple, leaving the couple inside the elevator to return to their rapture. Long, long kisses filled with timeless, hungry pleasure consumed them as his hands roamed avidly over her body. He explored the swell of her hips, the firm roundness in back, the slope of her shoulders, and the soft peaks of her breasts. She was entirely aflame, reveling in the strong, hard feel of him, and letting her own hands wander from the satiny skin at his open collar to the tight, narrow lines of his hips. The elevator bumped onward, carrying them at last to the very top of the building and opening onto a mercifully deserted hallway.

Ryan almost didn't notice that they had finally arrived, but his eyes caught a glimpse of the familiar wallpaper, and he grabbed her hand and led her out.

"This is it," he whispered hoarsely. "Thank God."

Jenny swallowed hard and followed him down the hall to a gray doorway marked PH. He quickly produced a key and opened the door, letting her precede him into the apartment. She caught quick flashes of color—gray carpet, maroon upholstery, beige lampshades—but neither one of them was interested in stopping now.

Ryan paused only long enough to turn to her, gazing somberly into her eyes. "I only know one thing right now, Jenny," he whispered, and his tone sent a little thrill coursing through her body. "I've never wanted anyone as badly as I want you."

She could only nod wordlessly in agreement, her mouth parted slightly and her green eyes shining with excitement. This time when he kissed her, it was with a deliberate slowness designed to prolong the buildup they had already created. Now there was no need to rush. His tongue met hers tenderly, weaving around it in a silky embrace that instantly ignited the sparks in her once again.

He led her down to the largest bedroom, carpeted in deep blue and furnished with a silvery art-deco motif. They stretched out across the huge bed that dominated the room, clinging to each other with all of the longing that had built up between them ever since they had met. Their clothes fell easily from their bodies, leaving nothing as a barrier and opening the way to the intimacy they sought. His mouth covered her breast in a sudden motion, charging her with a burst of desire that she never would have thought possible. Why did this one enigmatic, bewildering man conjure up such fire in her? Why, after all the careful years of planning and building her adult life, had he come along to effortlessly melt her into a pool of desire wanting nothing but him? But these thoughts were swept away under the tide that claimed her.

"Ryan, please!" she cried out helplessly, and his mouth began to move again. Lower and lower it moved, down the valley between her breasts, around and around her navel, over the slight womanly mound of her stomach, all the way to her very core awaiting him. With fleeting touches his tongue filled then emptied her, until she was whimpering with passion. She reached out blindly and found him, raking her nails over his back. His eyes turned to blue flames and he fell back, letting her overpower him as he had overpowered her. Her eager hands found the center of his manhood, delighting in the seeming paradox of silky smoothness and virile strength until he groaned hoarsely and slipped a restless hand between her thighs.

Her body opened readily for him, receiving him with a liquid rush of surrender. His movements were strong and slow, increasing gradually in intensity so that they rose together to a level of sensation that Jenny had never known before. She fluttered beneath him like a captive butterfly, beautiful in her passion and imprisoned in his grasp. Higher and higher they rose, until at last they were gripped by a showering of sparks that left them trembling in its wake. Bright patches of color floated by Jenny's closed eyes and she continued to hold him so tightly that her fingers were embedded in his skin.

"My God," he whispered in her ear. "What just happened?"

She couldn't answer, could do nothing but cling to him, holding on to the precious feeling she had discovered. After several minutes, she slowly released her grasp, and he slipped to her side. She nestled her head on his chest. Never had she felt so completely fulfilled.

She would have been content to lie there beside him forever. Both of them knew that something very special, almost sacred, existed between them now, and neither of them wanted to ruin it. It was still too new, too fragile to dissect, and so they let it drift over them, each hoping secretly that it would deepen and ripen on its own. But eventually reality brought them back to earth.

The digital clock next to the bed read 8:14. "Do you have plans for the evening?" Ryan asked gently, and Jenny giggled.

"No," she whispered back. "What did you have in mind?"

"Dinner. Are you hungry?"

She thought about it. "As a matter of fact, yes. I'm starved."

"Good." He sat up slowly and reached for the phone. "I'll make reservations."

Jenny found her way to the bathroom, stepping into the shower after a furtive glance around. Everything was utterly masculine—organized, simple, and large. Gratefully she surrendered her still-trembling body to the hot, steamy spray. A moment later the shower curtain was yanked open and Ryan stepped in.

"Hey!" she protested weakly. "Don't you know how to knock?"

He pretended to look offended. "You mean I'm not invited?"

Her eyes were luminous under the streaming water. "Oh, you're invited. You get to wash my back."

Half an hour later she was staring at him in astonished delight. "Well!" She beamed approvingly.

He looked down at his charcoal-gray suit, pale blue shirt, and striped tie. "What is it?"

"It's good to see you dressed in something from the twentieth century for a change."

"Oh, is that it? Believe me, no one on the street would give a second glance, no matter what I was wearing. This city is used to oddballs of every size and shape." He returned her frank stare. "You don't look too bad yourself."

"Thank you." She had chosen a simple but striking silk dress in navy trimmed with sleek kelly-green piping. Now that they were in New York, she was glad she had brought something elegant, just in case.

"Would you like to take a look around the apartment?" he asked, and she nodded.

Jenny's first impression was that it wasn't an apartment at all, but a house transplanted to the top of a skyscraper. She stepped into the living room, decorated in stark modern furniture, and stopped short when she caught sight of the picture window at the far end. The tops of other buildings and white wisps of clouds were set against the clear blue of the sky. It was almost like being in an airplane. But it wasn't just the view that created such a peaceful, serene atmosphere. There was a noiselessness, a timeless expanse in which the hurly-burly of the city below disappeared, leaving only this silent vacuum.

Jenny walked forward slowly, dreamily, to soak up the extraordinary sensation. From up here, Central Park looked like a solid mass of green, and the skyscrapers downtown were like silver birds taking off into flight. Straight down below, the people on the sidewalks moved steadily back and forth, and the traffic was a moving grid constantly trying to empty itself.

"I can't believe how removed this is," she breathed.

He came up behind her. "This is my escape capsule."

"More like a space capsule," she said ruefully. "Any minute now, we'll be going into orbit. No wonder you don't know what's going on in this city. You're never in it, you're above it."

"Maybe I like it that way," he answered.

She looked at him candidly. "Are you a recluse?"

"Of course not," he said impatiently. "Come on, I'll show you the rest of the place."

Jenny was amazed at the vast amount of space that was hidden away in an apartment building she would have guessed contained only the kind of tiny cubicles that were typical of NYC dwellings. The apartment had two floors—augmenting her first impression that it was more like a house—and it had a breathtaking terrace the size of the living room. Ryan led her through the spotless kitchen (she suspected it was spotless because it was seldom used), the elegant dining room, a cluttered study, and the two quiet bedrooms up the spiral stairs.

"It's a beautiful apartment, Ryan," she said sincerely.

"Wait," he said, holding up a hand. "There's more."

"More? Where?" She looked around, and he took her to another staircase that led to the sun deck on the roof. They stood in the rarefied air, listening to the whistling of the wind and watching the clouds playing tag. They looked close enough to touch, and once again Jenny felt that she was floating along on the wings of an airplane. A million tiny lights twinkled around them as the people of the city prepared for evening in the city that never sleeps. The breeze wound gently through Jenny's hair, and she shivered.

"You're cold," he said at once. "We'll go inside."

"No." She shook her head. "Not yet. I've never seen anything like this. I want to savor it and remember it forever." She spoke solemnly and he said nothing. "I had no idea New York could be like this," she added at last.

"It's not all like this," he reminded her. "This is an escape capsule, remember? The rest of it is enough to drive anyone crazy."

She turned away from him. "Oh, I don't know. It all seems so exciting."

Ryan smiled, watching her. "Slow down, country girl. We won't be here long. I'll keep my promise. Tomorrow morning we'll leave this vale of tears behind and head for Cape Cod. How does that sound?"

Jenny didn't answer, but her face reflected her sudden flash of doubt. She stared raptly at the city below, mesmerized by its almost tangible power. So far she had had only a brief glimpse of it, but she felt instinctively that its steady rhythm might be able to stimulate her and open up a part of her that had always remained dormant. "Let's go," she said.

The street brought a rush of sound and movement, making Jenny realize again how very removed they had been up in the clouds. The pulse of the city at night crept immediately into her system, creating an inner excitement and a subtle sense of rhythm. All at once the restlessness that had tugged at her for so long was dissipating. In its place was a new and delectable feeling of anticipation. She began to perceive that this city held some answers for her, but she said nothing as they got into a cab on Fifth Avenue.

"Tavern on the Green," Ryan said to the driver, and they drove off, heading into the darkness of Central Park.

Jenny thought they would exit again on the other side, but then she saw lights twinkling up ahead and the cab pulled up to a glittering restaurant that seemed to be situated right in the middle of the trees. The nearby branches were strung with tiny dots of white light, giving a fairyland atmosphere to the setting.

The restaurant was just as breathtaking inside. Sophisticated, expensively dressed people congregated around the bar, looking like cutouts from a glamorous magazine. Uniformed waiters careened expertly through the crowded tables, and the multitude of glittering crystal and gleaming silver continued the fairyland motif.

"Do you always eat at places like this?" Jenny asked.

He nodded wordlessly, and she could see that he wasn't particularly interested. They ordered drinks and Jenny looked around avidly, her eyes darting eagerly over the room.

"Looking for something?" he asked.

She nodded impishly. "I'm looking for celebrities."

"Oh, no," he groaned. "Don't do that."

"Why not?"

"It's . . . it's just a crass thing to do, that's all. Don't be such a small-town girl."

She tossed her head. "But I am a small-town girl. I'm not ashamed of it. Don't be such a snob."

"All right," he relented reluctantly. "But if you do see someone, don't stare."

"I'm not going to be rude," she flared. "I wasn't brought up in a barn, you know."

"I'm sorry." His smile was genuine, and she smiled back, fervently wanting the evening to be a success. "I guess I'm just a little edgy," he continued. "All that business with Lester makes me nervous."

"Why?"

"Because he's a manipulator. I've never trusted him, and I never will. I'm surprised he didn't drive a bulldozer into town, ready to tear up the place." Ryan sipped his drink angrily and looked away. "And all that phony-baloney Texas nonsense . . ."

Jenny's eyes widened in surprise. "Phony? What do you mean? He's not really from Texas?"

"Of course not. He moved there as a child, and now he thinks he's J.R."

"I see." Jenny watched him carefully. He certainly was touchy about the subject of his colorful relative. She had the distinct feeling that there was something he was not telling her, but she could tell that if she pushed him too hard or too suddenly, he might explode. "You did invite him to Great Barrington. And you also left him there to stew for a week," she observed.

He grinned. "That's right. He tried to railroad me into doing what he wanted with my share of the the inheritance."

All this was beginning to sound awfully childish to Jenny. She might be a small-town girl in the big city, but suddenly she felt much older and wiser than the sophisticated, wordly man across from her. "You didn't care what happened to your inheritance until very recently," she pointed out. "Sitting on that rock in the river really did change you, didn't it?"

"Oh, so we're back to that, are we?" Ryan looked decidedly uncomfortable, and Jenny was torn between her curiosity and the passion they had so recently shared. She didn't want to ruin the evening, but she didn't want to be kept in the dark about matters that affected her life. Thinking back, she recalled that Lester had never referred to Ryan as anything but his lawyer. Now she was even wondering what, exactly, that meant.

"You are Lester's lawyer, though, aren't you?" she asked point-blank.

"Of course. I was, that is. Not anymore. But that was because I was appointed executor of our grandfather's will. Until he died, Lester and I never knew each other."

"Really?" Jenny was stunned. "That's terrible."

He shrugged. "Lester was greedy. He wanted the house, the land—everything. It was my idea for my grandfather to give the house to the town. Actually, he wanted me—as the older, and, I might add, the wiser grandson—to live there, as a way of keeping up family tradition, but I wasn't interested, not then. I was too busy becoming a millionaire to worry about mundane family matters. I hadn't seen my grandfather in years."

"So what happened when you went to see him?"

"I didn't. He came to see me." He sighed, remembering. "It was right after my mother died. He always had rotten timing."

The waiter came with the wine, uncorking it with great ceremony and giving Ryan the first taste. "Excellent," he pronounced. "Let's get away from this unsettling topic of conversation, shall we? What about you? Tell me what it was like growing up in Great Barrington."

Jenny smiled shyly. "There's not much to tell. I'm afraid it was really very ordinary."

"I know." He beamed. "That's why I want to hear about it." He sipped his wine. "I ended up in New York by default. My parents split when I was very young, and my mother came to New York, bringing me with her."

"So you missed out on the all-American childhood in Great Barrington. Is that why you advised your grandfather to give his house to the town?"

He shrugged. "It held no memories for me. But as I was sitting on that rock yesterday, you came along, and suddenly I started thinking about what my life would have been like if my parents had stayed together and I had never left."

The waiter appeared to take their orders, and Ryan looked questioningly at Jenny. "Would you like to share the châteaubriand for two?" he asked.

She nodded. "Sounds delicious."

"Good." He turned back to the waiter. "Rare, please." The waiter glided off, and they were left alone.

Jenny watched him curiously, thinking about their fateful meeting. If things had been different all those years ago, she might have grown up with him. "You want to know about growing up in Great Barrington," she said quietly, and he nodded.

"All right. Here goes." She paused, thinking for a moment. "Well, everybody went to the same school, and there were very few secrets. It may have been small, but it was close. Do you know what I mean?" She glanced at him and he smiled his understanding. "Summer vacations didn't change things much. It was still the same group of kids."

"Tell me about the summers."

A slow smile lit up her face as she remembered. "They were sunny and long and beautiful. The nights were cool and misty, and in June the fireflies would light up the meadows like little torches. But the days were hot, and we kids spent a lot of time down at Race Brook Falls, in the cave."

"The cave? Sounds intriguing."

"Oh, it was. There was a huge cavern built into the rock, but the entrance was covered by a sheet of falling water. It was open only to the Secret Society, and of course I was a member." Her smile grew even more nostalgic. "All the kids belonged, and we thought the cave was our exclusive discovery. What we didn't know back then was that generations of children had discovered it, each one thinking they were the first." She sighed fondly. "I haven't been there in years. By now a whole new group must have found it."

His face was alive with interest. "Tell me more."

She chattered on, telling him all about her canoe trips on the Housatonic, her senior prom (during which she had jumped into the lake wearing her gown), her aunts and uncles, and her old collie, Smoke. The waiter brought their châteaubriand,

and she continued to talk excitedly, hardly aware of the time. "Mmmm, this is heavenly," she announced, tasting the succulent steak. "So anyway, Smoke and I were in the cave one day when Charley Barnett called out the secret password and marched in, followed by his friends."

"What was the secret password?"

She grinned impishly. "Oh, I don't know if I should tell you. We all swore in an elaborate ceremony never to repeat it, on pain of death."

"Oh, come on," he cajoled. "After all, if I had stayed there, I would have been a member of the Secret Society too."

"That's true," she allowed. "Well, all right. But you still have to promise never to tell anyone. I swear, if any of those people ever found out, even today, that I told you, they'd have something to say about it. Like I said, it's a close little community."

"Scout's honor," he said solemnly.

She leaned forward and whispered, conspiratorially, " 'As cloudy as the days may seem, Life is but an amber dream.' "

"What on earth was that?" He frowned.

"It was the last part of a verse that was embroidered on a sampler in the first-grade classroom. It was one of the first things we learned to read. I don't remember the whole verse, but it had to do with taking life as it comes and not taking everything so seriously."

"I see. Well, I won't tell. But what were you going to tell me about the day Charley what's-his-name walked in?"

"Charley Barnett. He was the local bully. He decided that from now on, girls weren't allowed in the cave. He and his friends tried to take it over, but Smoke jumped on him, and he gave up."

Ryan laughed delightedly. "I wish I had been there. I would have beaten him up myself."

"You still can," Jenny said, laughing along with him. "He now owns the town's male-only weight-lifting gym!"

Their laughter mingled pleasantly, and he poured the last of the wine. "Well, it all sounds like you grew up in a Norman Rockwell painting."

"You don't know how right you are. Norman Rockwell lived his whole life in Stockbridge, only a few miles away. We have one of his paintings, you know. It's hanging in your grandfather's study."

"Really?" he asked avidly. "Which one?"

"It's an early one portraying a group of boys at a swimming hole. I believe your grandfather actually knew Rockwell."

"He did," Ryan told her. "He mentioned it once."

Jenny was excited. "Just think," she mused, "if you had grown up there, you might have been in one of his paintings yourself."

Ryan sighed and nodded almost sadly. "That's true," he said. "Very true."

She finished the last of her châteaubriand. "That was worth coming to New York for." She smiled.

"Would you like dessert?"

"In a minute. I'm going to the powder room." She stood up, tossing her napkin on the table, and made her way through the elegant, brilliantly lit room.

Standing in front of the large mirror in the ladies' room, Jenny ran a comb through her wavy hair and freshened her lipstick. Her conversation with Ryan had intrigued her. He complained about New York, though he obviously fit here like a hand in a glove and his interest in her childhood had been sparked with the same curious intensity she had seen when he had confronted Lester. Could he actually be jealous? Of Lester? And, more incredibly, of her? She was the country girl, the small-towner, and he was the savvy lawyer who had made millions. She stared at her reflection, a look of wonder lighting her face. The glow had to do with more than the makeup she had so carefully applied.

A woman entered and stood next to her, patting her hair into place, but Jenny was too intent on her own thoughts to notice. Ryan Powers was an enigma, full of life and joy one minute, and brooding with dark impatience the next. And yet something seemed to be missing from his life, and Jenny couldn't help but realize that that something was invisibly connected to a secret and vulnerable place in her own heart. Was she falling in love with him? The thought was exciting and disturbing at the same time. There was so much about him she didn't know. And the memory of their lovemaking, only a few short hours ago . . . Her eyes closed for an instant as she relived the unbelievable sensations. When her eyes opened, she realized that she was trembling and that a tiny, breathless smile was darting across her face.

"Could it be possible?" she whispered aloud. "Am I actually falling in love with him?"

Her reflection gave her no answer, but the woman standing next to her did. She spoke up suddenly, in a startingly familiar voice. "There's only one way to find out," she said forcefully. "Go after him."

"Yes," Jenny replied, nodding thoughtfully, "I will." She turned to leave, but as she passed in back of the woman and reached the door, she was struck with the shock of recognition. Her head turned incredulously as she looked back at the reflection of the woman's vivid face in the mirror. The reflection stared back at her, the blue eyes radiant in their intensity. My God, Jenny gulped. Katharine Hepburn!

She couldn't stop herself from staring as she remained rooted to the spot. Miss Hepburn nodded encouragingly at her and then added a thumbs-up sign for emphasis. Jenny returned the nod and smiled, backing slowly out the door.

Chapter Six

"I want you to promise to say yes to something," Jenny said to Ryan as she returned to her seat.

He looked up from his coffee and she sat down, her face shining. She didn't want to tell him about Katharine Hepburn. He would never believe it—she could barely believe it had happened herself. It would remain her special secret.

"What is it?" he asked.

"First you've got to say yes." His suspicious look only fired her determination. "Come on, say yes."

"Well . . ."

"And you can't be angry," she added.

"Now, that's asking for trouble. What happens if I don't like it?"

"You'll like it, you'll see. Say yes." She looked at him beseechingly, but her eyes were dancing with merriment. "Please?"

"Don't rivet me with those beautiful green eyes." He laughed. "I tell you what. I'll say yes to whatever you want, if you'll say yes to something of mine. Is it a deal?"

Now it was her turn to hesitate.

"Taste of your own medicine?" he teased.

"No. I accept." She closed her eyes tightly, as if

waiting for an awesome surprise. "All right, what is it?"

"You first."

Her eyes opened and excitement colored her voice. "I want to stay here. In New York. I want to spend the week here instead of going to the Cape."

He stared at her with obvious distaste. "Are you crazy? New York isn't where New Yorkers spend their vacations. We leave in droves whenever we can."

"But I'm not a New Yorker."

"I was looking forward to a deserted stretch of beach on Cape Cod," he said a bit angrily, "not this madhouse."

"Yes. But you brought me here. And now I don't want to leave."

"Okay, fine. You can stay here if you like. Take the keys to my apartment and stay as long as you like. I'm going back to Massachusetts."

She pinned him with her gaze. "You promised."

"No, I didn't. You distinctly said that *you* wanted to stay here. It wasn't a requirement that I stay with you." He shook his head wearily. "I never should have left that rock in the Housatonic River!"

"Maybe," she said mildly. "But you can't hide all your life. And now here we are. Are you going to join me or not?"

He thought for a moment, and then his eyes gleamed, shooting little darts of steel. "I'll see." He sipped coffee. "I'll see. But don't forget. You owe me a yes, too."

She took a deep breath. "Oh, dear. What is it?"

His laughter rippled through her uneasiness.

"I'm not going to tell you, not yet. I'll tell you when I'm ready."

She frowned in protest. "That's not fair!"

"Of course it's fair. You can't add stipulations after the fact. A good saleswoman like you should know better."

"I'm not a saleswoman."

"Of course you are." He hailed the waiter and turned to Jenny. "Would you like coffee?"

"Tea, please. With lemon. But why do you say I'm a saleswoman?"

He looked mildly surprised. "I saw what you did with that museum. If that's not selling, I don't know what is. It must have taken a great deal of wheeling and dealing to put all that together. Not to mention the fund-raising!"

She looked down. "I never thought of it that way."

"Of course," he said impatiently. "I just hope they appreciate your talents."

"Thank you," she said softly. "And, yes, they do appreciate what I've been doing, only there isn't much more room for growth."

"Then it's time to leave," he said simply.

Jenny was astonished, not at the casualness of his statement but at its pinpointed accuracy. For months she had been wondering the same thing herself. Hearing it spoken so directly by him, it all seemed ridiculously clear. It was time to leave Great Barrington. And she was beginning to be very sure about where she wanted to go. She said nothing, however, except, "And I thought all I needed was a vacation."

He smiled, and once again she was struck by the

combination of intelligence and charm that emanated so easily from him. "That, too. Everyone needs a vacation once in a while, as I have recently discovered. I'm on vacation myself."

"Aha!" she cried. "I caught you! I thought you had retired."

"So I have," he acknowledged. "It's a permanent vacation." He ignored her annoyed glare. "We're not so very different, you know. We're just coming from opposite ends of the same candle."

"That's quite an image," she said dryly. "If we both keep on burning, eventually we'll meet in the middle."

"We already have." The blue eyes that missed nothing were twinkling at her over the rim of his cup.

"Dessert?" The waiter was standing next to them with the dessert cart. They turned and saw that it was laden with an awe-inspiring assortment of pastries and confections. "We have apricot-walnut torte, double fudge cake, chocolate mousse, lemon cheesecake, strawberries Romanoff, and plum tarts."

Jenny and Ryan pored deliciously over the choices and made their selections, lingering over coffee and liqueurs as the night progressed. Both of them carefully avoided the question of staying in New York, but Jenny knew that she would stay whether or not he agreed to join her. She simply had to unlock the answers she felt were here for her, no matter what her growing feelings for him might be. If she didn't stay now, she might never have the chance to find out. Ryan seemed to have his own questions to pursue, he clearly thought his answers were back in Massachusetts. Perhaps he was right. They had met in the middle of the same road, but were they only passing, or would they be able to stop?

At last Ryan looked at his watch. "It's late."

She nodded. "This was wonderful. I feel like a contented cat ready to curl up by the fire."

He called for the check, but when it came, Jenny surprised him. "Let me," she said.

"Oh, no," he protested. "I insist."

"But I want to. Please. This evening has been very important to me." She thought of Katharine Hepburn, and her resolve strengthened. "You don't understand, Ryan. I really want to."

"Well . . . all right," he said reluctantly. "If it means so much to you . . ."

She beamed and picked up the check, studying it before producing her American Express card. Everything was recorded carefully, but it seemed to her that the figures were added incorrectly. Mentally she did the calculations again and then hailed the waiter.

He appeared at once. "Something wrong, miss?"

She beckoned him over and pointed. "Are you sure this is correct? Shouldn't this be a five instead of a six?"

He frowned slightly and peered at the numbers, adding out loud. "No, no, miss. That's the figure from the bar added in." He did the addition with her, and her face changed as she realized her mistake.

"Oh, I'm sorry," she said deferentially. "I'm never any good at math. You're right." She took out her credit card and placed it on the table, shaking her head. "One of these days," she said to Ryan, "I'm going to take a refresher course in basic arithmetic. I always hated it." A mischievous smile crossed her face. "Of course, nowadays it's not necessary. I should just get a wristwatch with a calculator in it."

They both laughed and stood up to leave after Jenny had signed the receipt. "Back to my place?" he asked, and she nodded, knowing that soon she would be back in his arms.

But when they arrived at his building, the doorman handed him a telegram. "This arrived a few hours ago, sir," he informed him.

Ryan frowned and turned it over, looking for a clue. "Probably from a client," he muttered. "I haven't been too available the last few days."

They rode up in the elevator, and this time the trip was blessedly smooth and uninterrupted. It wasn't until they were standing in the apartment that he ripped open the telegram and read the message inside. Jenny watched his face change, filling suddenly with tension.

"What is it?" she asked anxiously.

"Damn that two-faced cowboy!"

"Lester?" she guessed.

"You won't believe what he's doing! He just couldn't wait. Monday they'll be moving in the heavy equipment. Construction workers will be there first thing in the morning. The nerve of him!"

Jenny was amazed. "But . . . so soon? How can he?"

"Legally he can do whatever he likes. And there's only one way I can think of to stop him." He threw the telegram down and ran into the bedroom, Jenny trotting after him.

"What? What are you doing?" she called.

He was already in the bedroom, dragging a suitcase from the closet and opening it on the bed. "I've got to get back up there immediately."

"But why?" she gasped. "Can't it wait until morning?"

"You don't know Lester," he answered angrily, throwing clothes onto the bed. "All my life he's been nothing but trouble."

"But . . . but you told me that you never even knew him until your grandfather died!" Jenny walked up to the bed, her hands on her hips. Ryan always reacted irrationally when it came to Lester, that much she had already learned.

"That's right, I never knew him. But he always managed to be a thorn in my side, even long distance."

She sat down on the edge of the bed and looked at him. "Don't you think you're overreacting just a little?" she said quietly, hoping to calm him down.

He stopped and looked back at her, his eyes turned to steel. "I thought you cared about this! Don't you realize that bulldozers could be tearing up that land of yours in twenty-four hours?" He began throwing socks into the suitcase.

"Yes, I do care," she answered. "But I'm not going to fly off the handle. All I'm saying is that you should think about this, and then make a decision. Running up there tonight won't do any good." Her forehead creased with worry. Although she had taken the role of the calm, rational one, even to the point of trying to reason Ryan out of his impetuous fury, she admitted to herself that she was disturbed by Lester's sudden move. She looked at Ryan curiously. He knew his cousin better than she did. Maybe he wasn't overestimating him. "Ryan," she asked, "are you sure you know what you're doing?"

He snapped the suitcase shut and came around the bed to stand in front of her. He pulled her up and looked straight into her eyes, his hands on her shoulders. "Believe me, Jenny, I'd like to stay." A moment passed before he kissed her tenderly, pressing her close for just a second. She curled her arms around his neck and tried to continue the fleeting kiss, but he wouldn't let her, his hands becoming strong suddenly as they gripped her shoulders. "But there's no telling what tricks Lester might have up his sleeve. He's been a weasel his whole life. You'll be glad I went." He smiled. "I might even end up a local hero. You can have my portrait added to the already illustrious Akins collection."

Her eyes fell. "What about your promise?"

He reached in his pocket and took out his key. "Here. You can stay here all week if you like. I don't know when I'll be back."

She took the key and fingered it rather wistfully. "You're so generous. First your car, and now your apartment." She didn't add that what she really wanted was him. But then she thought of something. Reaching into her pocketbook, she dug for her own set of keys. "Here you are," she said, pressing them into his hand. "You might as well stay at my place. Mrs. Olsen won't mind. Besides," she added with a wry grin, "I can't keep allowing you to stay in the pioneer house."

"That's true"—he grinned—"although I did enjoy it. Listen, make yourself at home here. After a whole week in this crazy city, you'll be more than ready to leave."

Jenny wasn't so sure, but she said nothing as he picked up the suitcase. She followed him down the hall and to the door. "Well," she said uncertainly, "Good luck with your cousin."

He blinked uncomprehendingly. "My cousin? What cousin?"

"Lester. Whom did you think I meant?"

His face opened in total surprise and the suitcase dropped heavily to the floor. "You thought Lester was my *cousin*?"

"Why . . . yes," she stammered. "Of course. The two Akins grandsons—you were in New York and he was always in Texas. . . . If he's not your cousin, then who is he?"

His mouth settled into a tight little line. "He's my brother."

Chapter Seven

The train rattled through the green hills of upstate New York, Jenny gazing absently out the window as she rolled closer and closer to home. Her week in New York had been packed with excitement and new experiences, but now it was time to go home and face the band. The countryside grew more and more familiar, but Jenny was busy reviewing all that had happened during the past eventful week.

First, there had been Ryan's strange departure. She still didn't know what had caused him to bolt so suddenly. And his final revelation at the door was equally baffling, especially since he hadn't given her much of an explanation. It was as if she was supposed to have known about him and Lester all along and was a blockhead for having been mistaken.

Brothers! She shook her head. It was still hard to get used to the idea. But anyone would have come to the same conclusion. After all, their last names were different. And they lived in two very different parts of the country, had different accents, life-styles, and values. Jenny had sometimes wondered how it could be possible that they were related at all. Ryan had only mumbled something about his mother reverting to her maiden name after his parents' divorce. Then he had sprinted off to the elevator and out of her life for a whole week.

She had tried to call him several times at her apartment, thinking more and more sourly each time how ironic it was that she was in his home while he was in hers, but there had never been any answer. All she could get were repeated, infuriating recordings of her own voice telling callers to leave a message at the sound of the tone. Whatever she had started up so rashly with Ryan Powers was definitely on hold.

Jenny turned her thoughts deliberately from Ryan—for the hundredth time that week—and focused instead on the eye-opening week she had had. New York was a city filled with contrasts, and although it could be both frustrating and confusing, it was never boring for a minute. The busy streets were filled with life and energy, overflowing with the spirit of hard work, far-reaching creativity, and old-fashioned hustle that made the wheels of this crucial city turn. Jenny wandered up and down the "Museum Mile" on Fifth Avenue, reveling in the internationally famous collections that spanned the scope of human history. She walked through miles and miles of galleries, overwhelmed by the treasures from every country on earth. When she wasn't basking in the wealth of the museums, she was browsing through the eclectic little shops that were tucked into every corner of the city. Hand-woven shawls from Bolivia, French cream flown in from Paris, Navajo jewelry, Victorian children's books, leggings from Iceland, newspapers in two dozen languages, Ukrainian Easter eggs—the offerings came from all over the world, to be crammed into this tiny island. Jenny discovered that it was not unusual to encounter a French hand laundry, a minuscule theater company, a dog-grooming salon, and a Hungarian restaurant all on the same block.

The sense of enterprise and activity floated almost tangibly on the air, entering Jenny's bloodstream with full force. On her fourth day in Manhattan, she decided to do something about it. Walking unannounced into the office of the curator of American art at the Metropolitan Museum of Art, she told the skeptical secretary that she wanted an interview. Her credentials and her obvious expertise got her inside, and she chatted pleasantly with the man for almost two hours. She wasn't exactly looking for a job and he wasn't hiring, but some instinct told her that this was a good contact and a good step. She left with a delicious feeling of confidence and ambition that she hadn't had since she had started her job in Great Barrington.

Every night she had returned exhausted but blissfully satisfied to Ryan's sleek but empty apartment. She couldn't believe that he could live in New York and never experience its unique pleasures. And she could barely remember the one trip she had made to New York years ago—a museum-hopping tour with a group of graduate students that had brought only crowds, noise, and aggravation. The New York she discovered on her own was the most stimulating experience she had ever had, and she didn't intend to let it remain as foreign as it had always been for her.

Every night she called her apartment in Great

Barrington, and every night there was no answer, only the frustrating answering machine. It was unsettling to be staying in his home, sleeping alone in his bed, and daily touching the things that were his when he had become so suddenly and inexplicably unavailable. It was easy enough to put him out of her mind during the days, when she was wearing out her shoes and filling up her mind. But walking by herself into his so-empty apartment each night would recall the memory of him in a rush, and sometimes she would fall asleep with her arms curled around his unused pillow.

Now, gazing out at the countryside as the train rolled into the Berkshires, she wondered again what she would find when she returned. Would Ryan be there at all? What would he be doing? She had to admit that she didn't know him very well, and he was unpredictable, to say the least. By the time the train stopped at Great Barrington, she was a bundle of confusion.

The first thing she did was to take a taxi to the museum, where her car was still parked. It had been only a week, but somehow the old Akins mansion looked different to her. Something had changed—or was she the one who had changed? Turning around to face the hills, she looked up anxiously for some sign of movement. Her heart sank. Sure enough, a small patch that had once been filled with trees was now cleared. Ryan had not been overreacting at all. Was he up there? She squinted into the sun, but no one was visible.

"Jenny!" Margie's effervescent voice came from the door of the museum. Jenny turned and saw her, her face lighting up with a smile. Margie was wearing a new dress and she looked extremely happy.

"Hi!" Jenny called back. "You look great!"

"Thanks." Margie beamed. "How was Cape Cod?"

"I don't know, I didn't go there. I mean it, Margie, you really look wonderful," Jenny said, walking up to the door. "I've never seen you so . . . so glowing." A conspiratorial gleam brightened her face. "I bet it's a man, isn't it?"

Margie said nothing, but her eyes gave her away.

"I knew it!" Jenny chuckled. "I can always tell. Spring is in the air and it's got you under its spell. So who is it? Anyone I know?"

Margie looked a little embarrassed. "Uh . . . not exactly. So if you didn't go to the Cape, where did you go?"

"Don't change the subject. Who's your heart-throb?"

"Listen, Jen, a lot has happened in the past few days. It's . . . it's kind of hard to explain. But the construction crews have been hired, and, uh . . ." She hesitated, and Jenny waited politely, puzzled. Margie was involved with a construction-crew worker?

"So who is it?" she prodded. "You can tell me."

Margie looked down. "Well, I guess you could say I've been fraternizing with the enemy."

"The enemy? What do you mean?"

"Look, Jenny," Margie began explaining in a rush, "this condo project isn't what we thought it would be. It's not so bad at all. Especially now that Mr. Powers is bowing out."

"Ryan?" Jenny asked quickly, her heart speeding up despite her best efforts.

Margie nodded. "They're only building a few hundred units and they'll be built right into the trees, with a fantastic view. We won't even be able to see them from down here."

"But what does all this have to do with your love life?" Jenny asked suspiciously.

Margie let out a heavy sigh and looked directly at Jenny with an air of resignation. "It shows that whatever Ryan may have told you about him is all wrong."

"All wrong about what?" Jenny asked with growing frustration. Then it hit her. "Lester? You're going out with *Lester*?"

"Did someone mention my name?" The unmistakable Texas accent came from inside, and a moment later its owner appeared. He strolled amiably up to Margie, and to Jenny's astonishment, he picked her right up in the air and gave her a big kiss. "How's my girl?" he drawled, setting her back down. Margie giggled furiously, and Jenny watched, perplexed. Lester turned to Jenny with a huge grin. Touching the brim of his cowboy hat, he said, "Howdy, ma'am. Nice to see you again."

Jenny mustered a weak hello as Margie looped her hand under his arm, holding on to him flirtatiously. "Well, well," she said, looking from one happy face to the other, "how long have you two been an item?"

"Well, I guess we got together after that meeting last Saturday morning, and we've been together ever since," Lester informed her. "You've done quite a job of keeping my grandfather's old place alive. I thought it would be filled with newfangled gear, but instead—"

"We've kept the *old*fangled gear, right?" Jenny broke in, and they all laughed.

"Right," Lester agreed. "The study looks just the way I remember it."

"I'm so glad. Was the Rockwell painting there when you were here?"

He nodded. "It sure was. Did Ryan tell you about that? He always was jealous about it."

"Jealous?" Jenny asked, trying to remain cool. "Why should he be jealous?"

"Because," Margie explained excitedly, "Lester is in the picture."

"What? You're kidding!"

They both nodded vigorously. "Yup," Lester said. "One of those kids in the picture is me."

"Now, don't tell me Ryan is the one in the background."

"No, he's not in the picture at all. That's why he's jealous. He never lived in this house, you see, but I did." Lester beamed proudly, and Jenny frowned.

"You did? When?"

"Until I was seven years old. Why, I even remember you."

"Me?" Jenny was amazed. "That's not possible. I . . . I'm afraid I don't remember you at all."

But Lester was adamant. "Sure you do. 'Jenny Moffat, eat your tuffet.' Remember that?"

"Oh, no," she groaned. "I haven't heard that in years. Don't tell me you were with—"

"Charley Barnett. He was my best friend. We almost took over the falls one summer." He began to chuckle. "No girls allowed. Little did we know how interesting those girls would become later on!" Margie squeezed his arm and he squeezed back.

Jenny was lost in thought, trying to remember. She would never forget that bully, Charley Barnett, but the rest of his gang had blurred in her memory. "I guess you're right," she admitted finally. "I still don't recall your face, and certainly not your accent, but if you say so . . ."

Lester let out a hearty laugh. "I didn't acquire an accent until we moved to Texas. When a boy is transplanted at the tender age of seven, he's still pretty impressionable. After twenty years out west, it's pretty hard to talk any other way. This here's the only way I know how." He flashed her a smile, and Margie nodded emphatically to back him up.

"I love your accent," she said cheerfully.

"But if you lived here until you were seven, when did Ryan leave?" Jenny asked.

"Right after he was born. He was just a little tyke in the cradle, cuter'n a bug. But things weren't running so smoothly at home. Our mother whisked him off to New York and they never came back."

Jenny nodded thoughtfully, and then tactfully changed the subject. "I'm glad you like our museum. Have you seen all of it?"

"I sure have. Margie treats it like her own home, and it sure is like a homecoming to me." He sighed nostalgically. "The memories come flying at me from every corner. You even kept the original silver collection in the dining room. That John Coney sugar bowl was purchased by my great-great-great-great-grandmother, you know, right from Mr. Coney himself."

"I know," Jenny answered, surprised. She had no

idea that Lester would know so much about the valuable art here, or that he would care about it in such a personal way.

"I'm so glad you noticed it," she said sincerely. Privately she was thinking that Lester wasn't so bad at all. He was more than a little colorful, but she was beginning to see why Margie found him attractive. He was really a very nice man. Of course, he didn't have his brother's magnetic sensuality, but maybe Margie saw him differently. What on earth was wrong between the two men? Why were they always at each other's throats? She decided to try to find out, delicately.

"May I ask you a question, Mr. Akins?" she began.

"Lester, ma'am. Just call me Lester."

"All right." She smiled. "And I'm Jenny. "Why do you suppose your brother advised you to go ahead with this building project?"

Lester looked a little surprised, but he answered gamely. "Is that all? It's pretty easy to figure out. He never cared about this place. He was happy to ruin it."

"But you accepted his judgment," she persisted. "When you arrived, you were the one who wanted to go ahead with it."

"That's right," he continued, a little too eagerly. Jenny could see the same irrational intensity in him that Ryan always had whenever he talked about his brother. "When he called me and said he had changed his mind"—he snapped his fingers angrily—"just like that, for no reason, I knew he had something up his sleeve. I thought he might just go in and do it all himself, cutting my share out of it. I wasn't about to let him get the best of me. He's a real fox, you know."

"Now, Lester," Margie said coaxingly, "don't get all riled up."

"I don't care," he fumed, gathering steam. "I can't help it. He's just jealous, and that's a fact."

"It seems to me," Jenny said carefully, "that you're both jealous of each other."

"What?" Lester was astounded. "Why should I be jealous of him? That greedy little money-grubber doesn't have anything I want!"

"Jenny . . ." Margie warned, but Jenny knew she was near the truth.

"Ryan is a good businessman," she said. "A very good businessman. Could it be that you admire his skill? Especially since he started with nothing and built his way up?"

"Don't be ridiculous!" Lester exploded. "He doesn't care about anything except money."

"I think he cares a great deal about this place," Jenny insisted. "Just as much as you do. I don't know how this whole condo thing ever got started."

"Well, no one is tearing up your precious museum, little lady, so don't you bother about that," Lester huffed. "I'm tired of being the villain in all this. You've got the wrong guy, believe me." He pointed up into the hills. "You won't even see the buildings from here by the time we're finished."

"I'm not accusing you, Lester," she said calmly. "But I do think you've got it wrong. Ryan isn't the villain either. I'm not sure anyone is."

Lester was growing more and more uncomfortable, Margie hanging firmly on to his arm, Jenny could see that she had needled him. Somehow she would get to the bottom of all this.

"What time is it?" Margie asked, trying to move away from this sensitive topic.

Lester looked at his watch and whistled. "My, my, it's late. I have to run. Can I drop you off somewhere, honey?" he said to Margie.

She shook her head. "No, that's all right." He leaned down and kissed her briefly. "We'll go on that canoe trip this weekend. You need to relax," she added softly. He kissed her again and turned to Jenny, touching his hat. "Nice seeing you again," he said stiffly, walking away.

There was silence for a moment between Jenny and Margie as they watched him go. "Well, imagine that," Jenny said finally. "You and Lester."

"You see, Jenny?" Margie asked earnestly. "He's not so bad at all, is he?"

"No," Jenny said honestly. "He's not." She smiled warmly. "In fact, he's very nice. "But I don't understand what he and Ryan have against each other."

"I don't either." Margie sighed. "They have nothing good to say about each other." She brightened. "But one thing seems sure. The development project has been reduced to such a small scale that we don't have to worry anymore."

Jenny nodded thoughtfully. "I wonder whose idea that was."

"Lester's," Margie said stoutly.

"Really?" Jenny looked at her sharply. "Margie, have you seen Ryan at all this week?"

"Yes, on Monday. Briefly. He's been up in the hills ever since, surveying." She shook her head. "Apparently he thinks Lester is trying to pull something off, and I know Lester thinks the same thing about him. They've been busy figuring out the boundaries between their land."

"You know something?" Jenny mused. "I think they're both wrong."

Margie smiled a little sadly. "Maybe. In any event, it sure has livened things up around here." Her smile became mischievous. "I have a feeling you've had a pretty lively time yourself."

"Why?" Jenny asked suspiciously.

"Because you got a very interesting phone call from a Mr. Gordon Howard of the Metropolitan Museum in New York, that's why. He said something about wanting a regional consultant."

Jenny's face lit up. "He called? Really? When?"

"Whoa, slow down." Margie laughed. "He called first thing this morning."

"So you knew I didn't go to the Cape!"

Margie spread her hands. "I didn't know where you went. But that call this morning was a good clue."

"So what else did he say?"

"Nothing." Margie shrugged. "He just left the message."

Jenny could barely hide her excitement. "I'll have to call him right back." She dashed inside the building and up the stairs to her office. But when she eagerly dialed the New York number, she found that Mr. Gordon Howard wasn't in.

She hung up, disappointed, but Margie was watching her curiously. "You must have had quite a week," she said.

"I did." Jenny nodded. "I walked my feet off and loved every minute of it. But it looks like I missed some interesting action back here." She paused, hesitating. "Uh . . . so you saw Ryan Powers, did you?"

Margie's eyes gleamed. "Yes, but as I said, he disappeared up into the hills. Why, Jenny? Is something going on between you two? I saw the sparks flying last week."

"Let me put it to you this way," Jenny said with a hugh sigh. "Guess whose apartment in New York I've been staying in all week?"

Margie's eyes widened. "Ryan's?" she gasped. "This is getting more interesting by the minute."

"Of course, Ryan left rather precipitately," Jenny added dryly. "When he got Lester's telegram, he rampaged out like a tiger with a singed tail."

Margie sat down and they looked at each other. "You know what I think?" Margie asked.

"What?" Jenny said cautiously. Margie sometimes had rather startling ideas that were creative but not very practical.

"I think we should get those two guys together." Margie sat back with an air of satisfaction. "All they need is a little push."

Jenny shook her head firmly. "We can't interfere in their personal affairs. We might be playing with a keg of dynamite."

"Look, Jen," Margie said persuasively, leaning forward, "Lester and I are going on a canoe trip this weekend. Couldn't you and Ryan just happen to come along? It's a group trip. There will be lots of people there. Maybe they'll relax and have a good time."

"Well . . ." Jenny was torn. She hadn't been canoeing yet this season and it certainly sounded tempting. The truth was that her hesitation came from her uncertainty as to whether Ryan would accept her invitation, or whether she would even be able to talk to him at all. "I'll see," she said finally. "I'll see."

"What is it, Jenny?" Margie asked kindly. "You look a little down."

"Oh, it's nothing, Margie," Jenny hedged. "I'm just wondering what Ryan Powers is doing in my life, that's all." It came out more bitterly than she had intended, and Margie looked at her sympathetically.

"Don't tell me you're in love with him," she said softly.

Jenny didn't answer, and Margie whistled. "That bad, huh?"

"Now, don't jump to conclusions," Jenny said impatiently. "I didn't say anything."

Margie held up a hand. "I tell you what. We'll take this quiz."

"Oh, no. What quiz?"

"There's a quiz in this month's *Rendezvous* magazine—'Are You in Love?' " She fished in her desk. "Here it is."

"Come on," Jenny protested, laughing. "That's not going to solve anything."

"I know," Margie said impishly, "but it will be fun. And you never know, maybe it will help."

"Oh, all right," Jenny agreed. "You read me the questions and I'll answer them."

Margie whipped out a pencil and a piece of paper, and opened the magazine to the right page. Sitting back importantly, she read in a serious voice, " 'Are You in Love?' Question one. 'If he gave you a birthday present and you hated it, would you: A) tell him the truth nicely, B) pretend you liked it, C) exchange it?' "

Jenny thought for a moment. "I guess I'll have to say A," she answered.

Margie's eyebrows lifted, but she made a notation on the paper and read the next question. " 'When he kisses you, are you thinking of: A) him, B) an old boyfriend, C) a fantasy lover?' "

"Well, A, of course," Jenny said flippantly. But she was thinking of the long, slow ride up the elevator. Every time she remembered it, it sent chills up her spine. Thinking of someone else! Fat chance!

Margie read the next question. " 'How much do you think of him? A) all the time, B) on and off during the day, C) only at night?' "

"Uh . . . I'll say B," Jenny answered, squirming a little. Little did Margie know she had been thinking of him right then!

"Good. 'How long did it take you to answer question three?' "

"Why?"

"Because that's question four."

Jenny almost laughed, thinking that the whole thing was rather silly, but Margie was waiting earnestly. "Well, right away, I guess," she said.

The next question was surprisingly prophetic. " 'If he goes out of town for a week, do you: A) cry into your pillow every night, B) miss him but carry on, C) go with someone else?' "

Jenny sighed. "How coincidental," she muttered. "Well, I'll say B."

They continued down the list of questions, and Jenny answered dutifully, Margie checking off her responses. "Okay," Margie said when they had finished. "That's it." She handed Jenny the answer sheet. "Now, you get three points for every A answer, two points for every B answer, and one point for the C's."

Jenny calculated quickly and looked up. "I got twenty-two," she announced. "What's the verdict?"

Margie read from the magazine. " 'Lukewarm. You are strongly attracted to this man, but you're not sure if your feelings could be classified as love. All in all, something is missing.' "

"What's missing is him."

"What?"

"Enough conjecture. What's missing is the man who inspired this quiz in the first place." Jenny crumpled the piece of paper and threw it toward the wastebasket. "I'm going home, Margie. I've got to find Ryan and discover my own answers." She stood up and strode to the door.

"Good luck!" Margie called after her.

Jenny ran out to the parking lot and jumped into her car. It was time to stop avoiding her feelings about Ryan. But one thing was for sure. That quiz had been wrong. Lukewarm was definitely not how she felt. Now that she was back in Great Barrington, she couldn't wait to see him again. Knowing that he was somewhere nearby made her tingle with anticipation.

She drove home as quickly as she could, passing by the place in the river where she had first seen him. The rock sat placidly, and she almost expected to see him sitting there, but he wasn't. She drove on, parking in front of her house, where Mrs. Olsen was busy tending the garden.

"Hi, Jenny!" she called out as the car pulled up. "Welcome back."

"Hello, Mrs. Olsen. I . . . I hope my friend wasn't any trouble."

"Who?" Mrs. Olsen frowned. "Oh, you mean that nice fellow who's been staying in your place. Oh, my, no. I never even see him. He's no trouble at all. I hardly know he's here."

"Really?" Jenny asked carefully.

"Why, I've never seen such a hard worker," the landlady chattered on. "Up at the crack of dawn and heading out every day to work on that land. He works late, too. Last night I saw his light on way past midnight."

Well, that was interesting news. At least she knew Ryan was really here. But it sounded like he was back to his old habits, working around the clock. "So he's come out of retirement at last," she mumbled.

"What was that?"

"Oh, nothing, Mrs. Olsen. I'll just go upstairs and unpack." She lugged her suitcase up the stairs and then remembered that she had given her key to Ryan. Calling down for Mrs. Olsen to let her in, she waited nervously, wondering when she would see him.

Mrs. Olsen bustled up the stairs and opened the door. They both stepped inside and gasped. "Oh, my God!" Jenny exclaimed. "It looks like a tornado hit this room."

The usually neat living room had been turned into an office, but it looked like the office of an army's headquarters. The furniture was strewn with survey maps and equipment, legal volumes, building ordinances, graphs, blueprints, accounting sheets, and photocopies of the local paper dating back to the nineteenth century. She noticed a copy of Josiah Akins' will lying on the table, and one map with red pins stuck into it at various points was tacked haphazardly to the wall.

Jenny stared aghast at the scene and then ran over to her answering machine. Just as she had suspected, the volume control had been turned off. No wonder he hadn't answered her calls. He hadn't even heard her messages. She rewound the message tape and played it back. Most of the calls were from her.

"Everything all right, Jenny?" It was Mrs. Olsen, who was still standing in the doorway.

Jenny sat down in the middle of the mess. "Yes, I'm fine, Mrs. Olsen. It's just that I think I'm in love."

Her landlady's eyes twinkled. "Aha! But you're not sure."

"Actually," Jenny said wryly as she got up and dusted herself off, "it's kind of hard to say. You see, I only scored twenty-two on the love test. That means I'm lukewarm." Ignoring the older woman's puzzled look, she skipped down the stairs and went back to her car.

If the mountain won't come to Muhammad . . . she thought, sprinting off, leaving a trail of dust behind. Ryan was up in the hills somewhere, and it shouldn't be too hard to find him. All she had to do was look for the surveying equipment. Back on the river road, she passed once again by the famous rock where they had first met. Only this time she caught sight of a familiar car. She slammed on her brakes. "I don't believe him," she said to herself, her heart thumping. "Now he's back to meditating." She got out and walked over to the riverbank, wondering nervously what she would find and what kind of greeting she would get.

Ryan was perched on the rock exactly as he had been that first day. Only this time he was dressed in jeans and a denim jacket, and his leather boots were safely above the water line. A pair of binoculars hung around his neck, and he looked up pleasantly when he saw her.

"Hi, there," he said cordially.

Hi, there? That was all he could say after disappearing for a week? How was she supposed to respond to *that*?

"Uh . . . it looks like we're back to where we began," she said rather tartly. "Only this time you're looking a lot more chipper."

"I am, I am," he assured her. He took the binoculars from around his neck and held them out. "Come and have a look. I spent the whole week surveying my land, and now it's all mapped out."

"That's nothing to get excited about," she answered crossly. She stifled a sigh. This wasn't going at all the way she had wanted.

He smiled. "Oh, yes it is. It seems my grandfather had some special plans that none of us knew about. Come on over and take a look."

"I'm not going into that river," she said fearfully. "The water is freezing."

"No, it isn't. Come on, or I'll come over there and carry you." To confirm his words, he stood up and began to make his way through the water.

"Is this really necessary?" she protested. "Can't I just look from—"

But before she could finish the sentence, Ryan had lifted her solidly in his arms and was carefully wading his way back to the rock. When he got there, he sat down and placed her soundly on his lap. Jenny squirmed a little, but in her heart she didn't really want to protest. She had been thinking about him all week, and now she was sitting here with him as if nothing at all had gone wrong. The river smell wafted pleasantly around them, a contrast to the city smells she had so recently experienced, and Ryan's strong arms were wrapped protectively around her.

"There," he said, obviously pleased. "Now I have a captive audience." He handed her the binoculars. "Look over there," he said, pointing up into the trees.

She followed his directions, sensing his excitement. Automatically adjusting the lens, she scanned the hills and waited for him to continue.

"Lester can't build any condos," he said gleefully, "not with this arrangement. I've found a way to stop him. Just look over there."

Jenny looked. "Look for the red flags," he said, guiding her hand. "They mark the borders between my land and Lester's."

She perused the hills for a minute, using the one cleared patch as a focal point. Then her eyes slowly traveled, down until she saw a red flag. "I see one," she said, feeling an inner sense of suspense.

"Good." Ryan held her firmly. "Keep looking."

"I am."

"Now slowly move to the left or the right. It doesn't matter which."

She continued along until she spotted another flag about twenty yards away. "What—?" she started to ask, but Ryan gently coaxed her on. She found two more small flags, all at similar intervals. "They seem to be just moving in a circle around the hill," she said finally, looking back at all the flags she had found.

"That's right." He beamed.

"So," she said perplexedly, lowering the binoculars, "what's so exciting about that?"

"Don't you see? My land completely encircles Lester's land. His is on the top and mine is on the bottom."

Jenny didn't know what he was talking about at all. "So what?" she demanded. "Why is that important?"

"Because Lester can't get to his land without going through mine! I've got him surrounded. Now do you understand?"

"All I understand," Jenny said grimly, "is that you have yourself worked into a frenzy over this whole foolish thing. If you and your brother would just—"

"Oh, Jenny," he broke in angrily. "You don't know what you're saying."

"I know exactly what I'm saying. You've been hiding up here like a madman all week and you've been working yourself to death. All that talk about retiring was ridiculous. You'll never retire. There will always be some project to keep you busy around the clock. If you're not squabbling like a child with your brother, it will be some other battle." She said this all in a rush, as her face turned crimson with frustration, but she wasn't at all sorry. She meant every word.

"What are you talking about?" he shouted, gripping on to her. "You were so upset about your precious land last week that I promised to do something about it. And now that I have, you're totally ungrateful!"

"*My* precious land!" she sputtered, trying to wriggle free. "I seem to recall that over dinner last week, you were very interested in this area. You wanted to hear all about your lost childhood, as if this were some kind of never-never-land. Maybe Lester is right about you. Maybe you did advise him to go ahead with the condo project just to spite your own family."

His anger rose swiftly, his hands digging into her. "You were the one who had to stay in New York all week. All of a sudden you weren't interested in the Berkshires anymore."

"I never said I wasn't interested," she said peevishly. "It's just that you were more preoccupied with your crazy relationship with your brother than you were about anything else—including me. You didn't even call me all week long. How do you think I felt?"

"What do you mean, I didn't call you?" he demanded. "How do you know I didn't call you?"

"Because I never heard from you, you idiot!"

"Well, for your information, I tried to call. Several times. But you were never in. I wasn't even sure if you had stayed in my place."

"And I wasn't sure you had stayed in mine!" she countered just as harshly.

"Wait a minute," he broke in, his tone calmer. "You tried to call me?"

"Yes," she admitted. "I . . . I needed to talk to you."

"Don't you see?" he said, turning her so that she faced him. "I was up here all week. I never knew that you called."

"That's hard to believe," she said petulantly. "What about the answering machine?"

"What answering machine?" he asked blankly. "And where were you all week?"

She began to laugh weakly. "I was out running around, just like you were."

"So we've missed each other all week," he concluded.

Her head grazed his shoulder. "I certainly missed you," she said shyly. It wasn't what he had meant, but it didn't matter.

"I missed you, too," he whispered into her ear, holding her close. "I didn't know how much until just now. But now that you're here, so deliciously close . . ." His words trailed off as he kissed her, like an explorer just returned from a long, hard journey. It wasn't exactly the answer Jenny wanted, but it would do for now. Hungrily she returned the kiss, letting her tongue wind its way smoothly around his. She forgot her doubts and her confusion as she lost herself in him. Nothing mattered except that she was back in his arms. She should have realized it would come to this. All the analyzing in the world meant nothing when he was touching her like this. A slow, contagious fever grew between them, deepening as his hands slid through the silk of her hair and roamed further to capture the delicate swells of her breasts. Jenny moaned softly and knew she was lost. She would do anything to prolong this tormenting pleasure.

Ryan's touches were like little jolts of electricity. Suddenly a week apart seemed like an eternity. She didn't know how she could have lived through it, how she could have existed without this stingingly sweet passion in her life.

"Oh, Jenny," he whispered, his voice thrilling her with its intensity. "A whole week . . ."

Tears stung her eyes as she realized that this moment meant as much to him as it did to her. She rested her head on his shoulder and clung to him, her eyes tightly closed. Every fiber of her being was singing on a single line of desire.

"Jenny . . ." He lifted her head gently and looked at her.

She couldn't answer, but only looked at him, her eyes shining.

"Let's go." His voice was quiet, but she heard the longing in it.

He picked her up, holding her closely, and waded carefully to the shore. But when he set her down again, they realized that they were confronted with two cars.

"Yours or mine?" she asked.

They chose his and he drove swiftly to her house. The silence between them was an intimate one, intense but comfortable. When they entered her apartment and closed the door behind them, Ryan took her in his arms and looked directly into her eyes. His own eyes were a searing blue, the lines of his face engraved with passion. "How I want you," he murmured.

Jenny's eyes closed at the wave that washed over her. He lifted her up again and carried her to her bed, letting his body fall over hers as he set her down on it. They sank together into the softness, Jenny waiting with trembling anticipation for his tender assault. His arms were crushing her against him as if to meld her into his body, and his mouth was claiming hers, branding her with flames that made reality spin away. Time simply stopped for them, and every movement, every touch, became an indelible memory. Ryan's hands played delectably with the lines of her back, which were moving constantly under his spell, and when they traveled around the seductive curve of her waist to find her breasts, she tugged at her clothing to ease his way. It seemed he couldn't possess her fast enough, and she wanted nothing except to surrender. His mouth closed on the rosy tip of one breast, bringing it to fullness. Jenny's eyes closed luxuriously as the warm tide rose within her.

"Sweet Jenny," he murmured softly, his head moving down. Tiny, fiery kisses were planted all down the length of her body. Her legs opened unconsciously as he left a delicate, dizzying trail on the insides of her thighs, and her back arched, ready to meet him. Ryan sat up and struggled hurriedly out of his clothes, Jenny helping him through the haze of her passion. Her hands could not stay still; they curled around the square lines of his chest and dropped to cradle the center of his manhood with feathery touches that rendered him utterly helpless. Jenny reveled in the power she had over him, knowing that it could break at any moment if he chose to end it.

He ended it by uttering a cry that was strangely savage. She fell back, overcome, and he enveloped her immediately, his knees between her long, sleek legs. They joined together in exquisite, tormenting slow motion. Jenny trembled vibrantly under him, her body molding itself around him. Their rhythm increased in spite of their efforts to control it, and each movement brought them nearer and nearer to the pinnacle they sought so desperately but wanted to delay. Wild colors flew by Jenny's closed eyes and she saw, as if from a great distance, that the end was very near.

But he spoke to her, his voice coming from a great hollow depth. "Look at me." Her eyes fluttered open and looked into his, and she saw the same profound craving that was lodged in her heart.

When it was over, after they had tumbled over clouds and fallen back down, they nestled lazily in each other's arms. It was one of those delicious moments in which everything and nothing is relevant, but filtered through the layers of contentment, Jenny remembered something.

"Ryan . . ." she whispered.

He kissed the top of her head. "What?"

"I want you to promise to say yes to something."

There was a dangerous pause.

"Ryan?"

"What?"

"Will you? Say yes?"

"Again?" he asked. "That's not fair. I haven't even used up my yes yet."

"All's fair in love and war," she said lightly.

"Oh, all right," he agreed reluctantly. "Now, what is it?"

"First say yes," she insisted.

"Yes," he said. "Yes, yes, yes, yes."

"Good. Then tomorrow morning you and I are going on a weekend canoe trip down the Housatonic River." She stopped, waiting for him to explode.

But he didn't. "Is that all?" he asked.

"That's all. Now, that wasn't so bad, was it?"

He answered by sliding his arms under her body and kissing her. "Was it?" she repeated.

But he was in no mood for conversation. He claimed her again swiftly and she complied with all the force of the swelling emotions she had for him. She knew he would never have given her a straight answer. He rarely had a straight answer for anything. And that was exactly what scared her. Because the answer in her own heart was becoming loud and clear.

Chapter Eight

"It's almost eight o'clock," Jenny mumbled sleepily, nudging Ryan gently with her toe.

"Mmmm," he answered, snuggling down into the covers. Jenny didn't blame him for being so drowsy. He had reached for her again and again during the night, and neither one of them had gotten much sleep.

Jenny started to hoist herself out of bed, but he reached out and grabbed her arm, pulling her back down. "Hey," she said weakly, but he threw a lean-muscled leg over her satiny one and pinned her down. "We have to leave," she said.

"Not yet," he whispered with lazy determination. His hand trailed across her skin until it found her breast, and he held its firm softness gently, teasing the nipple awake. Jenny could hardly believe that she could respond so easily after the night of passion they had shared, but once again her senses were flowering into arousal.

"There's no time," she tried again, but he answered, "This won't take long." With swift, sure motions he coaxed her body into awareness, and before she knew it they were entangled in the demands of their desire.

Then the phone rang, shattering the magic. Jenny groped for it and swallowed hard. Ryan tried to stop her, but she grabbed the receiver.

"Hello?" she croaked. "Oh, hello, Margie. Uh . . . no, it's not too early. Yes, yes, we'll see you there." The receiver clattered back into its cradle, and she jumped up before Ryan could stop her. "We'll have to hurry," she said, ignoring his murderous look.

She dressed quickly and went into the kitchen to prepare a big country breakfast. She knew he probably didn't eat much breakfast as a habit; black coffee was probably his usual fare. This would be a good change for him.

By the time he entered the kitchen, clad only in a pair of faded jeans, coffee was perking merrily, English muffins were in the toaster oven, a batch of scrambled eggs was cooking, and a bowl of fresh blueberries was sitting on the table.

"What's all this?" he asked curiously.

"Breakfast," she answered. "What else?"

He surveyed the food with amazement. "You eat all this in the morning?"

"I knew I was right. Sit down."

He sat, and she served the eggs and brought in the muffins. "Go ahead"—she nodded—"dig in. I'll just get the orange juice."

"Oh. There's more?"

She laughed and he joined in weakly. "Eat," she commanded, and he ate.

"That was delicious," he said with real surprise twenty minutes later.

"Of course." She beamed, clearing the dishes away and taking them to the sink. He followed her and stood next to her, his arms folded across his bare chest.

"Hmmm," he said, fingering the strap of her bikini top under her T-shirt, "this should come off easily when we're alone in the bushes."

She gave him a wide-eyed look. "This is a group trip," she said pointedly. "There will be lots of other people there." She didn't add that Lester would be one of them. If she told him now, he might refuse to go altogether, in spite of his promise. Glancing nervously at the clock, she quickly took care of the dishes and prepared to leave.

The drive to the launching point was strangely silent, as if Ryan knew what awaited him. Jenny was suddenly anxious, but he would find out soon enough by himself. Maybe Margie and Lester would come late, so she would have a chance to prepare him. But as they pulled up at the launch site, she spotted Margie's car parked nearby. With a distinct sense of foreboding, she got out and followed Ryan to the small group of people gathered around a large, husky man.

"You're just in time," he greeted them jovially. "We'll be leaving right after I give some basic instructions. My name's Tank, by the way. Now, you folks go on over and get yourselves a canoe." He gestured toward a large truck, and they saw a stack of canoes being unloaded.

They started walking over, when Ryan stopped short. "What the hell is he doing here?" he demanded rudely.

"Now, Ryan . . ."

He wheeled, his eyes boring into hers. "Did you know about this? Did you know he would be here?"

Lester turned, his cowboy hat towering over everyone else's heads. A slightly sinister smile was on his ruddy face, and Margie edged toward him nervously. "What's the matter, Ryan?" he asked evenly.

Ryan bit back whatever he had been about to say, and the two men backed off. The group leader ambled over hastily and held up his hands.

"Now, I'll need to know a few things before we take off," he announced. "Do all of you have experience handling white water?" Everyone nodded, and he looked specifically at Lester and Ryan. "You two gentlemen are new here, so I want to ask you both."

"I have," Ryan said stoutly. "On the Lehigh in Pennsylvania."

"So have I," Lester added quickly. "But it was on the Colorado, not the Lehigh." His tone was tinged with just the slightest touch of condescension, and Jenny and Margie exchanged looks.

"Well, good," Tank said sternly. "I don't want anyone ending up in the water. It's pretty cold this time of year." He looked the group over. "Now, in case any of you are a little rusty, I want to remind you that the first thing you do when you hit white water is to back-paddle. Aim backward against the current to keep control of the canoe." He lifted a paddle and demonstrated. "Everybody understand?" There were affirmative responses. "Okay," he concluded after several more instructions, "let's get started. We'll launch the canoes one by one and travel down the river single file."

The group broke up and the canoes were carried down to the riverbank. Soon the first few pairs were afloat, but Jenny and Margie held back. Lester and Ryan were eyeing each other warily as the last two canoes were carried down.

"You knew I was coming, didn't you?" Ryan said suddenly to Lester.

"Only shortly before you did," Lester answered. "But I was just as surprised as you were, believe me. I didn't think you'd be interested in canoeing. Not any more interested than you are in what happens to the land we inherited."

"I really don't know what you're talking about," Ryan said coolly.

Lester searched for a suitably irritating reply, but looked up to see Jenny and Margie paddling the next-to-last canoe in the river. "Hey!" he shouted. "What do you two think you're doing?"

"Canoeing!" Jenny yelled back. "And I suggest you and your brother join us, unless you want to be left behind."

"Oh, hang it all," Lester exclaimed. "I knew that little troubleshooter had something up her sleeve."

"Well, come on," Ryan said irritably. "Let's go." The two men pushed the last canoe into the river and jumped on, Ryan in the stern and Lester in the bow. They managed to catch up with the others, but it was obvious that neither one was pleased with the other's company.

"I suppose you two think this is funny!" Lester called over to Jenny and Margie.

"On the contrary," Jenny called back. "It's high time you two learned to get along."

"And you'd better learn fast," Margie added. "The rapids are coming up just around the bend."

They all looked up, and sure enough, the

rushing sound of white water could be heard. The first few canoes were already bouncing into the rapids, expertly steered by the most-experienced people. Jenny and Margie maneuvered efficiently, working together as a team, and their canoe was jetted smoothly along before bumping into the white water. "Here we go!" Margie cried, steering deftly around a rock. The hazards loomed ahead, and they handled them, one by one, making instant decisions with excellent reflexes. They wove around piercing rocks, angled logs, and sudden whirlpools, the sound of the water in their ears and the fresh, clean smell of it tingling their noses as the spray rushed across their faces. The fast water ended as abruptly as it had begun, and all at once their canoe was on serene water once again. They laughed triumphantly, pleased with their first maneuver.

"Great job," Jenny commented, turning around to watch the last canoe come through.

Ryan's voice could be heard as he shouted at Lester. The canoe careened wildly at the first drop, and Margie frowned worriedly. "They'll never make it," she said.

Jenny didn't know whether to laugh or sympathize. "Just listen to them."

"Steer!" Lester hollered. "Steer, can't you?"

"Back-paddle, you fool!" Ryan yelled back. "Back-paddle!"

The canoe dived menacingly through the rapids, looking as if it couldn't make up its mind whether to sink or swim. The two men paddled furiously at cross-purposes. By now the entire group was watching with a mixture of amusement and concern. Somehow the brothers made it through, and they both looked decidedly relieved when they sailed safely onto the smooth water.

"You idiot," Lester said to Ryan. "I thought you knew how to steer!"

"I do," Ryan retorted, "but I can't when you're floundering around like that!"

They were so busy arguing that they didn't watch where the canoe was going, and it turned sideways, its nose pointing toward the bank. Before they knew what was happening, white water was upon them again, and they were being tossed headlong into its midst.

"Steer!" Lester screamed frantically, trying to gain control of the canoe. His paddle was useless against the current, and he succeeded only in turning the canoe all the way around. They were now flying backward, completely helpless in the furious backwash. Their angry shouts and accusations were to no avail. The canoe hit a bump, and the two men were thrown unceremoniously into the cold, rushing water. A second later, they were rising to the surface of a broad, motionless pool. The canoe bounced in after them, its furious bucking instantly halted as it arrived safely in the clear water.

Tank, the group leader, paddled hastily to the shore and leaped out of his canoe. "Are you fellows all right?" he called out.

"We're just fine," Lester spluttered, coughing up water.

"Are you sure?" Tank called dubiously.

"Of course we're sure," Ryan broke in angrily. He swam to the shore with a few strong strokes and climbed up. Lester followed him quickly, and the canoe floated lazily after them.

"Can't you do anything right?" he hollered. "I don't believe how a bumbling lawyer—"

"Oh, shut up, you phony cowboy!" Ryan roared back.

Jenny and Margie silently witnessed this exchange. Margie looked embarrassed and unhappy, but Jenny's patience suddenly snapped.

"Stop it, you two!" she said fiercely. "If you can't resolve your foolish differences, then at least don't air them in front of us. We're not interested!"

The two men ignored her, glaring at each other as rivulets of water streamed from their clothing. Jenny was furious. Had it been only yesterday that she had thought she was in love with Ryan? "Stop it!" she commanded. "What have you two got against each other?"

The tension hung in the air as Ryan and Lester launched their canoe again and continued on without a word. Jenny looked straight ahead, knowing that a repeat performance could erupt at any moment.

But there wasn't time to worry about that. Ahead of them, a huge wall of water was churning ferociously, driven by the rocks and eddies underneath, and the canoes at the head of the line were disappearing into it. As the threatening cloud swallowed their colleagues, they prepared to follow, bracing themselves for the onslaught.

The roar of the water drowned out all other noises, and they knew that their shouts would never be heard. Jenny said a silent prayer as she and Margie entered the violent mist. She hoped that

Ryan would watch the path that her canoe would carve. She had navigated this river many times and knew all of its tricks. It was hard to remember her first bout with it, but she knew that it had not been easy. Veering almost automatically to avoid a large boulder, she expertly guided the craft to safety. She was afraid to look back, but when she did, a surprise awaited her.

Just as she had hoped, Ryan had observed her course and was following close behind. Lester, to his credit, was steering carefully, concentrating on following the narrow path. They made it around the boulder and stopped, parking in a natural eddy.

The rest of the group broke into friendly applause, and Tank called out, "Much better, boys. I want to see you keep up that teamwork."

Jenny said nothing, but her eyes sparkled with satisfaction. If getting dumped in the river could teach them how to get along, then that was fine with her. "Let's let them continue on their own for a while," she said to Margie in a low voice. Margie nodded and they paddled vigorously ahead. Jenny turned to peek at the two brothers out of the corner of her eye.

"How are they doing?" Margie asked. "Are they talking?"

"I can't tell," Jenny replied. "It's up to them."

Margie couldn't deny the truth of that, and they glided peacefully down the river, drifting slowly into another world. Civilization now seemed very far behind them as the long branches of the trees cast long shadows over the shimmering water. They stroked rhythmically, listening to the incessant calls of the birds and the little lapping sounds made by their paddles as they dipped in and out of the flowing river. Jenny closed her eyes for a breathless moment, inhaling the earthy freshness of the air and absorbing the bountiful peace. Behind her there was only quiet.

At lunchtime the group pulled into a small alcove, and for the first time Jenny and Margie saw that the brothers were actually conversing. In fact, they seemed to be hatching some kind of conspiracy. They spoke together in rapid, covert whispers, and when Jenny asked what they were talking about, they both looked at her with knowing grins.

"Well, whatever it is," Jenny said sagely, "I'm glad to see it. That wasn't so difficult, now, was it?"

"Not at all," Ryan agreed heartily. "We just made ourselves a little deal that should make both of us happy."

"That's wonderful." Margie beamed happily. "Then everything is . . . working out?"

"Couldn't be better." Lester nodded, taking her hand. He led her over to a patch of grass, where they bit hungrily into the sandwiches that had been prepared.

Ryan and Jenny sat together with their feet dangling in the water. She was still unconvinced, but decided not to press him. It was his business, after all. They finished their sandwiches wordlessly. Ryan put his arm around her and gave a little squeeze, but she lifted her hand and tried to dislodge it. He responded by grabbing the hand and holding it tightly, and she tried to yank it away. She expected him to pursue it, but he didn't. He dropped his arm and gave her a strangely cunning smile.

"What is it?" she asked involuntarily.

"You'll see."

"Are you and Lester. . . ?"

He didn't answer. Standing up and stretching, he said only, "Let's go."

The first few canoes were already back in the water, and the remaining ones were being launched. Jenny walked up to Margie and said, "Let's switch seats this time."

"Good," Margie answered. "I'd like to steer."

Jenny climbed into the front of her canoe and took up her paddle, waiting to begin. But she was disconcerted by Margie's shout of surprise.

"What are you doing?" she demanded. "You tricked us!"

Jenny wheeled around just as her canoe jolted forward. Margie was still standing on the shore, and it was Ryan who was powerfully pushing the canoe into the river. He jumped into the stern and began to paddle, sending them swiftly into the current.

Jenny turned all the way around and glared at him. "So that's what you two were hatching back there!"

He didn't bother to hide his triumphant smile. "I didn't come along on this trip to be with Lester. I came to ravish you in the woods, remember?"

Jenny wasn't paddling, but Ryan was masterfully keeping the canoe on course. "No comment?" He grinned. "Well, even if you have nothing to say, I do hope you'll contribute your talents soon. I hear the rapids up ahead are pretty dangerous." Jenny began to paddle reluctantly. "I'm the one who should be angry, you know," he continued. "You had no right to trick us into going on this trip together, let alone in the same canoe."

Jenny was thoroughly confused. As put off as she was by Ryan's attitude about his brother, she realized now she had wanted him to come on this trip so that she and Ryan could have some time together, not because she was trying to interfere in his relationship with Lester.

"I hope you're wearing a seat belt," Ryan called out merrily. She knew he was just baiting her, trying to get her to talk. But she barely knew what to say. If he could only know how much she wanted to be close to him, to understand what drove him so hard. After a week apart, it was desire that had brought them together again, not the intimacy she yearned for. And as strongly as the desire burned through her defenses and flooded her with an indescribable craving, she knew that ultimately it was not enough.

She could hardly say all of this to him now. As much as his inexplicable antipathy with his brother caused a barrier between them, she would gladly tolerate it if only he would try to explain it all to her.

The next series of rapids came up after a few more silent minutes. Jenny found that Ryan handled them deftly, and she began to relax. They steered skillfully through the churning water, ducking swiftly at one point to avoid a low-hanging branch, and then the river opened into a broad, peaceful passage.

"Why don't you just sit back and let me steer for a while," Ryan suggested. "I'll enjoy the activity."

She decided to take him up on his offer; she lay back in the canoe, squinting up into the sun. His powerful strokes carried them downstream, the rhythmic dipping and lapping of the paddle lulling her into dreamy complacency. She knew that the next two hours of the river were slow and easy, and as long as he stayed with the rest of the group, there was no cause for concern. The tops of the lush trees glided by overhead and an occasional bird flew across her field of vision. After a while she fell into a restful doze.

A splash of cold water on her face revived her, and she awoke with a jerk. They were going through another brief series of rapids, and Ryan was handling them perfectly by himself. He gave her a sardonic smile as she turned around to look at him, the afternoon sun reflecting off his face and giving his hair a decidedly reddish tinge.

"It's past three o'clock," she heard the group leader call as they bounced into the deep, quiet water again. "And we're approaching a nasty series of rapids that forks up ahead."

Devils and Angels, Jenny thought to herself.

"It's called Devils and Angels," Tank continued. "The left fork is called Angels, because the ride on that side is smooth. That's the side we're taking, in case you've got any doubts. The other fork is called Devils, and if you take that one, it's at your own risk." His tone was jovial, but Jenny knew that he was serious.

Ryan was looking to the left and to the right. "There it is," he acknowledged. "The left side is as smooth as glass, and the right side looks hellish." Jenny caught the glint in his eye. Oh, no, she thought. Don't even try it. Just go to the left like everyone else.

"Did you say something, Jenny?" She shook her head and huddled back down in the canoe. The rhythmic lapping started to calm her again, but then the canoe started to bounce. The water was getting rougher. It was too rough, she realized, looking up at Ryan in alarm. His face was perfectly composed; perhaps this was just a little rough spot on the Angels side that she had forgotten about. But the sudden roar of sound was much too loud for it to be Angels. Her thoughts were interrupted by a sudden rude bump that almost lifted her right off the bottom of the canoe. It was followed by another bump and then another. Her face telegraphed silent alarm, but still Ryan was placid and unconcerned. He certainly seemed to have things under control, but something was wrong and she sat up to look.

It was as though a blast of dynamite went off in her head. Her whole nervous system reacted, charging her with energy. "You idiot!" she screamed, struggling up to her seat in the bow and grabbing her paddle. The canoe was rocking furiously from side to side and she had to fight to keep her balance. She knew that water like this would require the strength of both of them if they were going to make it through.

"Glad you decided to join me," he called out.

She whipped around and saw the same sardonic gleam in his eye. But there was no time to argue as they took a sudden dive down a perilous drop.

"Back-paddle!" Ryan commanded, and she did, bracing herself with all of her might. She pushed fiercely against the frenzied current as the canoe began to drop down a four-foot embankment of streaming water. It was the start of what was to be the longest forty seconds of her life.

Chapter Nine

"Back-paddle!" Ryan yelled.

"I am!" she screamed back, but she knew he couldn't hear her. The spray whipped into her face with such force that she was blinded for a second. Then she perceived a blurry object straight ahead and she forced the bow of the canoe to the right. "Watch that rock!" she shouted.

The canoe nosed down steeply and water poured inside of it, but Jenny barely noticed. They careened toward a tree that was growing right in the middle of the water, narrowly avoiding a jutting rock that protruded in front of it.

"Duck!" Ryan called over the roar of sound. The low branches grazed the top of Jenny's head as they maneuvered past it and then down another dizzying drop that ended in a maddened whirlpool of swirling white water. She could barely see through the thick mist that sprayed around them, but a thunderous sound told her that a waterfall was up ahead.

"Back-paddle!" she heard him shouting.

But his voice was lost as the white mist clouded up into the sky, blotting out the sun for one breathless split second in time. Then, as if in a dream, a multicolored rainbow appeared at the bow of the canoe. It was unearthly in its beauty, and for a moment Jenny could not believe her eyes.

There was no visibility whatsoever now, and they shot along blind at a breakneck speed. Back-paddling was useless in this storm. At one point the river narrowed sickeningly, sending them shooting through a churning canal.

"Almost there!" Ryan called as they whipped around a jagged boulder, but the thunderous sound ahead was becoming even louder, and Jenny knew that the worst was still to come. "Oh, no!" he cried, realizing what lay ahead.

Now they could see the enormous drop only twenty feet away. The canoe arched upward in an enormous wave, and she looked around wildly for an alternative passage, but there was none. She thought she saw their group over on the other side waving and pointing and calling, but it didn't matter. They now had only one destination, and it was inevitable.

"Get ready!" Ryan yelled. "If we make it, we're home free!"

Jenny back-paddled until her arms felt like paper. She realized that it was useless to paddle at all against such an onslaught, and she ducked low, grabbing hold of the sides of the canoe. A huge gush of water rained over them, but she felt no rocks underneath and breathed a silent prayer of gratitude for that. Peeking over the edge of the canoe, she saw the rim of the drop. It was smooth and glassy, surging forth majestically at a thirty-degree angle and emptying into a swirling pool that led to yet another drop. Suddenly, at the last possible second, Ryan anchored the stern with a sharp pull that sent the bow up into the air. Jenny screamed—half in excitement and half in terror—as the canoe flew through the air over the rushing water. It was as if some imaginary force had grabbed the second hand of a clock and stopped it from moving forward. She had the illusion of flying in slow motion, and the curious sensation fascinated her even as she held on for dear life. The roar was deafening, and for a moment she felt that she was inside of the roar itself. Suddenly the sun showered hot rays that shot through the mist and Jenny looked down at ten feet of beautiful cascading water. They were suspended in time, motionless, and then they snapped back to reality. The canoe angled down with the falls, the impact of pressure causing a tremendous shock as water poured over the hull and filled the craft like a tub. The ice-cold, clear water hit Jenny in the face like a knife, stinging her with its intensity. The canoe sliced through it all, hurtling through the rapids, until at last, with one final surge of speed, they found themselves gliding through the tail of the rough water into blessedly smooth current. They landed with a soft bump in a mound of mud that was embedded in a little alcove.

Jenny closed her eyes, opened them, and breathed a long sigh. She turned around, half-expecting to see no one in the stern, but he was there grinning at her like a Cheshire cat. "Well," she said. "So. Does this mean we're even?"

He panted, still out of breath, the grin hanging on his face like a half-moon. "I'd say I overdid it this time."

"Are you two all right?" a distant voice called, and Jenny saw Tank waving at them from across the little island that separated them. The rest of the group was applauding and cheering and Jenny and Ryan waved back.

"We'll camp here tonight," Tank announced. "If you two would like to join us, just paddle on over. We'll be eating dinner in about an hour."

Ryan waved again in acknowledgment and stepped out of the canoe, checking the waterproof bags to make sure they were still intact. Everything was in good condition, and he smiled, helping Jenny onto the bank of the little island. Her gait was suddenly unsteady, as if she could collapse now that she had been tested and had passed.

"Easy there," he said encouragingly, holding on to her arm.

She tried to glare at him. "You like risks, don't you?"

He held her steady and looked down into her eyes. "It's the story of my life." He smiled a little, but his smile was serious. "We both needed it, Jenny. Face it. You were getting bored."

"If I was," she answered, leaning against him, "that little escapade has cured me for life."

"Me too." He looked around. "Now, I think we deserve a reward, don't you? Tonight we'll have a little privacy. We'll sleep here, on this island."

She knew better than to argue. Her own longing coupled with the hair-raising experience she had just had made her want to curl up in his arms and stay there. Ryan took out their sleeping bags, unrolling them in a little clearing, and they both reached for warm, dry clothes.

Jenny shivered as she climbed out of her wet jeans. She practically had to peel them off. Her T-shirt clung to her body like a second skin, the chill bringing her nipples to firm peaks. Ryan took off his shirt and tossed it down. Their eyes met. Jenny dropped her glance at once, but he strode over to her and touched her arm, letting the warmth of his hand soothe her. "Come here," he whispered. Both of his hands combed through the long tresses that were plastered to her shoulders, and he tilted her head back. Jenny was keenly aware of the group of people only yards away, but they were hidden by the trees and she knew it was useless to protest. His kiss was warm and comforting at first, but almost at once it became demanding, sending fire through her blood. She pressed against him, her cold, damp breasts finding refuge in the shelter of his chest. He lifted the T-shirt over her head and threw it on the ground, taking her breasts firmly in both hands. She was wearing nothing but white lace briefs, and he caressed her body hungrily, with maddening butterfly strokes. The long, deep kisses continued, sending that wild, familiar craving like an electric current between them.

"Jenny!" Margie's voice filtered through their passion like a call in a dream. "Are you all right?"

They broke apart reluctantly, still clinging to each other as Jenny called back, "Yes, I'm fine! Just a little wet!" She was out of breath, and she shivered suddenly, a tremor of cold passing through her body.

"You're cold," he whispered, rubbing his hands on her bare arms. "We'd better get dressed."

She nodded wordlessly and donned a clean pair of jeans and a pullover sweater. When she faced him again, he had put on a plaid shirt and a denim jacket. Quickly she ran a comb through her damp hair, and then turned to go.

The rest of the group welcomed them with cheers as they paddled up in their canoe. "You two gave me quite a turn," Tank said cheerfully, "but you handled it as well as anyone could." His eyes twinkled. "Are you hungry?"

The smell of succulent steaks sizzling on a crackling fire made Jenny realize how hungry she was after her ordeal, and she nodded.

"I thought so. Dinner will be ready soon. Why don't you just relax for a while? You've earned it."

Tank went to join the rest of the group, which was lounging casually around the huge pit, one of the men tending the steaks. Tents were pitched all around the little cove, and it looked like a strange little suburban community of canvas dwellings, each with its own front yard.

"I like our little hideaway," Jenny murmured impulsively to Ryan as they sat down together on an old tree stump.

"So do I," he whispered back.

The sun flickered low behind the trees, casting long golden rays on the river. There was a cool, velvety feeling in the air, and they watched as a family of birds fluttered into their nest, chirping excitedly. Someone brought out a guitar and began to strum, and a few people joined in singing rounds. Jenny snuggled against Ryan. His arm went comfortably around her, drawing her close, but immediately she felt it knotting with tension. She looked up to see him staring fixedly at Lester and Margie, who were exchanging a kiss as they emerged from one of the tents. Jenny smiled a little, but Ryan's scowl warned her that something was wrong.

"Ryan," she pleaded. "Promise me you won't start anything. Not now."

"Me, start something? Me?" He looked at her curiously. The passion they had shared a few minutes ago was gone, replaced by a new mood of bitterness. "I don't believe that son of a—"

"Ryan!" Jenny warned. "Please, don't spoil things tonight."

"Spoil things!" he repeated, turning to face her. "Now I know what your problem is. You think that I'm perpetrating some kind of family feud! You don't know how wrong you are."

"I don't care," she protested. "I'm tired of hearing about it, whatever it is. Honestly, I've never seen such childish behavior. Jealousy doesn't become you."

"Jealousy!"

She stood her ground. "Well, what would you call it exactly?"

A sudden realization seemed to overcome him and he shook his head. "Tonight, when we're alone, I'll explain it all to you. Everything," he added emphatically.

"What's to explain?" she asked. "Sibling rivalry is as old as the hills."

"Very poetic," he said dryly. "But this isn't sibling rivalry. It has nothing to do with Lester being my brother." He sighed. "Don't you think I'd like to regain the family I never had?"

His plaintive words surprised her. He had never

spoken like this to her before, and he sounded as if he thought she had understood some secret of his.

She wanted him to continue, but a familiar voice from behind stopped them. "Well, howdy there, bronco riders."

They looked up and saw Lester and Margie seated on a nearby rock. Lester was holding his cowboy hat carefully in both hands, the way one would hold a fragile cake. They all watched as he twisted a sturdy stick into the ground and then hung the hat on the stick. "My lucky hat," he said with a confidential air. "It got a little waterlogged back there on the river, but this fire should dry it out nicely."

"The water must have taken away some of its magic charm," Ryan said meaningfully. "I think your luck has just about run out."

"Ryan . . ." Jenny warned under her breath. "I thought we agreed."

Ryan said nothing, but she could feel the tension being held in check. Lester ignored him and pulled Margie close, giving her a little nip on the ear. But when he caught Ryan's scowl, he pulled back and looked away. It was as if Ryan were sending him some sort of silent command. Even Margie felt something amiss and she tried to pull him back.

"Uh . . . come on, Lester," she said with a manufactured smile. "Let's . . . let's go and get a cold beer."

Lester looked as though he hadn't heard her at all. He stared back at his brother, open challenge reflected in his tanned face. "Is this the way it's going to be, little brother?" he asked coldly, his voice low.

Ryan started to say something, but stopped himself.

"Oh, I get it," Lester continued, baiting him. "The silent treatment. You stay on your side of the fence and I'll stay on mine. Well, that suits me just fine. You mind your own business and I'll stick to my own affairs."

"An apt choice of words," Ryan commented brittlely.

Lester was finally nettled. He pushed Margie's arm away and glared at his brother. Jenny was startled, and Margie swallowed hard at seeing his obvious priority.

"You can think of me any way you want," he said, pointing a finger at Ryan, "but hear me out. I never lose in any business deal I invest in. But even if I do, that's my problem now, not yours."

"Business?" Ryan growled. "Who said anything about business? I'm talking about—"

"I know damn well what you're talking about. And it is none of your business!"

Ryan let out a short, hard breath and smiled coldly. "You know something? You're right." Lester looked suspicious, and he went on, "It doesn't matter now. You almost made me forget that I already have the solution, and I'm going to stop you once and for all. By next week I'll be seeing you back to Texas—for the last time."

Margie turned a questioning gaze to Lester, her alarm apparent. Lester looked sharply at Ryan and then tried to smile at her. "Uh . . . honey, why don't you go on over there and bring me a nice cold beer?"

"But—"

"Go on, now. You don't want to get mixed up in this."

Margie got up reluctantly, hesitating.

"Don't make such a big deal of it, Margie," he added convincingly.

She gave him a faltering smile. "Well, all right." When she was safely out of earshot, Lester dropped the remnants of his facade. "Now, look here, buddy," he said to Ryan. "You can't stop me. You never could, and you know it."

"Oh, yes I can," Ryan answered hotly, his anger rising to the surface. Jenny could tell that he was beyond calming words, her pleas for peace driven out of his head by Lester's baiting.

"How?" Lester challenged, with all the confidence in the world.

"All right, I'll tell you. I was going to save this for a better time . . ." He looked at Jenny, but even she was curious, wanting him to continue. "Listen carefully, old buddy. You know that surveying I've been doing all week?" Lester nodded in spite of himself. "Well, it's been very revealing. You might be interested to know that your half of the land is all on top of the hill."

"So what?" Lester shrugged. "It's the better half. It has the view."

"Maybe so. But the bottom half is mine—all of it, all the way around. In short, you'll have to go through my land to get to yours, unless you plan to use a helicopter." Ryan spoke quietly, but the force of his words was not lost on them.

Lester looked as if he was about to explode. His face was purple and he stared at his brother with undisguised animosity. "Why, you—"

"It wasn't my idea," Ryan broke in mildly. "It's all there in the will, if you look for it."

"But, Ryan," Jenny spoke up, "why can't you work with Lester? He's reduced the condo project so that it won't interfere with anything. He told me we won't even be able to see it from down in the valley." She looked at Lester for confirmation, but he ignored her.

"Is that what he said?" Ryan asked gently. She nodded. "And you believed him?"

"Why?" Jenny asked, as if she already knew the answer.

"Have you seen his plans?" he inquired. "His blueprints?" Jenny shook her head, her face filled with consternation. "I'm afraid you'll be in for a very unpleasant surprise when you do. He's planning a whole spread up there. It looks like the plans for a suburb. It's got everything, including a shopping center." He shook his head distastefully. "Believe me, it will be anything but invisible."

Jenny confronted Lester directly. "Is this true?"

He squirmed, avoiding her gaze. "Well, I . . . it's not that simple," he hedged.

"Don't try to weasel your way out of this," Ryan warned. "It's bad enough the way you're carrying on with poor Margie, but—"

"What do you mean?" Jenny asked, frowning. "Surely that's not for you to judge." But she had a sinking feeling that there was more to it than that, even as she tried to defend her friend. "I'm sure Margie knows what she's doing."

"And I'm sure she doesn't." Ryan's eyes were on Lester's.

"I told you to mind your own business," Lester

retorted. "Maybe you can cause trouble in the land deal, but my private life is my own affair."

"Again, a sadly accurate choice of words," Ryan said dryly.

Jenny's face suddenly flooded with comprehension. "You mean he's . . ." She turned to Lester. "You're married!" Lester's silence confirmed it. "Oh, my God!"

They were interrupted by a startled sound, and they looked up to see Margie standing there with a cold can of beer in her hand. She turned an open, earnest face to Lester, but he wouldn't face her, and she knew that it was true.

"You low-down . . . How could you?" she cried. "I had no idea!" Tears sprang to her eyes, but pride forced her to keep them in check. Lester's angry scowl was for Ryan, and he showed not the slightest hint of remorse.

He tried to grab Margie's hand, saying in a honeyed tone, "Aw, come on, honey. What difference does that make? I thought you wanted to have a good time, just like I did."

Margie was practically speechless in her anguished fury, but she managed to choke out, "You . . . you make me sick!" Her fist was clenched and her face was a mask of rage. "You . . . you . . ." She looked around wildly, as if searching for the words to express her indescribable feeling of betrayal, and her blazing eyes focused suddenly on his. In one swift, furious motion, she grabbed his hat from its resting place and tossed it into the fire. Then she turned and ran off, as the hat filled with smoke and slowly burned to a crisp.

Chapter Ten

As Ryan lit the small campfire he had built in front of their tent, Jenny looked through the trees of their island enclave and caught a glimpse of the flames from the larger fire across the river.Free from the diffusing glare of city lights, the stars twinkled luminously in the black sky, studding the darkness with shimmery light. The crescent moon shone like a proud queen over it all, and the gentle whisper of a breeze stole through the trees.

"What a romantic night," Jenny said softly. Ryan nodded in agreement, watching as the flames darted between the pieces of kindling. "But I'm still worried about Margie."

"She'll be all right," he said stoutly.

"She didn't have much of an appetite at dinner."

"I know. But these things take a little time. And she's no shrinking violet." He chuckled quietly. "I almost laughed out loud when she threw Lester's stupid cowboy hat into the fire."

Jenny couldn't help but smile. "Did you see the look on his face? It was as if someone had tossed in a . . . a . . ." She searched for an analogy, but Ryan broke in.

"A stack of hundred-dollar bills." They both laughed this time.

"Oh, Ryan," she sighed, "why didn't you tell me Lester was married?" She still found it hard to believe.

"It never came up, that's all," he answered, somewhat surprised. "Besides, these things aren't of paramount importance in his life."

"You mean he's done this before?"

Ryan said nothing, but the look of distaste on his face gave her the answer. "But I didn't know he had been fooling around with Margie," he said after a pause. "I guess I was too busy all week to notice anything." He took her hand. "But I've been noticing a lot of things since you got back."

"Oh, really?" She smiled. "Like what?"

"Like the look on your face," he stated matter-of-factly.

"Me? What look?"

"That look of contentment. New York gave you something you sorely needed, didn't it?" He nodded sagely. "I knew it would." He looked through the darkness of the trees and sighed. "I was an idiot for bringing you there."

"But why?" she demanded. "I had a fabulous time. If you hadn't brought me there, I never would have known."

"Known what?" he asked, a note of fear in his voice. "That you don't belong here anymore? That you want to live there instead?"

Her face dropped in surprise. "Is that what you think?"

"I think it's a distinct possibility," he admitted. "Why should that surprise you?"

She hesitated, unwilling to reveal this final truth. "Because it's true," she said at last.

Silence prevailed for a long moment, during which they stared into the fire.

"But . . . is that so bad?" she continued awkwardly.

He sighed impatiently. "I told you, Jenny. I've had it with New York. I want to move here."

"I don't believe that." Now it was her turn to be impatient. "You'd get bored in no time at all. Just look at how you spend the last week—working!"

"Yes. But I was working here. Not there."

"I don't think that makes any difference," she said slowly. "And I seem to recall that you did enjoy New York very much when you were there with me."

Ryan smiled a little. "You're right. Maybe there's hope for me yet."

"Of course I'm right. You just needed a little vacation, that's all."

"And a pair of fresh eyes," he added, drawing her close.

Jenny closed her eyes, relishing the warm, strong feel of him as he held her. Her head rested on his shoulder, her long pale hair streaming down her back like a cloak. The week that had just passed darted across her mind, a moving kaleidoscope of impressions.

"I went to every single museum," she whispered. "They were wonderful." Then she remembered. "I went to see the curator of American art at the Met."

Her whispered words dropped like a small bomb.

"And?"

"Well, I don't know. But Margie said he called yesterday."

"What did he want?" Ryan asked impatiently.

"Something about wanting a regional consultant. I don't know exactly. But I'll find out."

"And if they offer you a job, will you take it?"

"How should I know?" she asked, exasperated. "I don't even know what it is. Why should you care?"

His eyes glinted, but he said nothing. She couldn't tell what he was getting at. He was the one who had suggested she try her wings, but now he was snapping at her for no good reason.

"Look at me, Jenny." He cupped her face in his hands and looked deeply into her eyes. He seemed to be demanding something from her, but the strange intensity that always marked him when something was troubling him was there now. His eyes were a deep blue in the starlight, radiating two tiny pinpoints of light. Jenny wanted to reach through the wall of intensity more than anything in the world. She wanted to melt the steel in his eyes, to gentle him with her touch, to find her way into the secret places in his heart. But she was afraid to try, afraid that he would withdraw if she got too close. And as always, the desire was there, spiraling up between them like a lush, cabled vine. It mingled delicately with her own straining heart, creating a profound yearning that gushed over her like a waterfall.

"Ryan . . ." she whispered, searching his face, silently pleading with him to bridge the gap, to take the step forward and let her meet him halfway.

He heard the longing in her voice and ran his hands down the sides of her face to her shoulders, stopping for a fleeting second before lightly drawing two lines down her arms. She shivered involuntarily, her hands curling under his touch, the desire pounding within her like a caged animal. "Kiss me," she breathed, and he did, the warmth sending a beacon of light through her body. His hands lifted the weight of her hair, fondling it luxuriously before letting it fall again. Their tongues met easily, tasting of wild honey.

Jenny shivered again, trying to press herself against him. "Come," he whispered, taking her hand. They snuggled down together into his sleeping bag inside the little tent, still dressed except for their shoes. He pulled her close quickly, holding her against the night's chill, raining kisses on her face, her neck, and burrowing his face onto her shoulders and beyond.

He sat her up and removed her sweater. Her skin was silky under the rough material. The small bra unclasped in the front. She unhooked it and let the flimsy straps fall down her shoulders. It fell on the ground as his mouth traveled around one trembling mound, firm yet impossibly soft. The fire in her was like a bolt of electricity. All he had to do was touch her to reach its deepest source. She moaned when his mouth settled on the pink tip of her breast, teasing it into fullness. Suddenly she needed to feel him against her. Her hands tugged at his jacket, pulling it off, and fumbled with the buttons on his shirt. They held each other greedily, reveling in the shock of her satiny skin crushing against his smooth, hard chest. Her breasts yielded and then rose as he squeezed her and let her go, leaving a little pocket of air between them so that he could continue his journey down the glowing lines of her body.

He unsnapped her jeans and slid them down over her long, slender legs. His own jeans came next, and soon they were burrowing down into the sleeping bag, tingling with anticipation.

Ryan's hands explored the shadowed recesses of her body, lighting fires wherever he touched her. "Love me," she pleaded, and although he obliged her feverishly with all of his inspired skill, she couldn't help wondering if he knew that she meant more. The intensity in him had metamorphosed into passion, but she knew it must still be there. Desperately she sought to cut through it, and her hand dropped to return his caresses. A deep masculine groan of pleasure escaped him. They aroused each other with excruciating tenderness, delaying the final surge of passion as long as they could. He kissed her stomach, his hands molding the swell of her hips, and her legs opened of their own accord. The warm kisses descended to the delicate insides of her thighs, his tongue flicking teasingly until she twisted luxuriously beneath him. Her body carried the clean, earthy scent of the river, and it was the sound of the river flowing past their island that mingled with their breathless whispers.

"Oh, Jenny," he cried in a blaze that thrilled her. "You don't know what you do to me, do you? I want you, all of you, now!"

As if she could have resisted, she thought helplessly. She was ready to give her very soul to him, if only he would have it. His body covered hers, his knees between silken legs that had gone weak with longing.

There was a moment of delicious anticipation, both of them knowing that their passion was about to be fulfilled. His entry was slow and deliberate, but her body was so ready for him that they joined together in a silken, liquid rush.

"Oh!" she cried.

"Tell me," he whispered savagely. "I have to know. Tell me you want me just as I want you."

"Oh, Ryan, don't you know?" she answered him, as she savored him filling her, completing her. "I want you . . ."

His hardness commanded her and led her into a wild dance. She struggled to keep up, moving with him as she clung to him. Their rhythm increased, causing her reason to slip away from her, out of control, as she lost herself to him. Her entire mind and being focused on the central core of passion that united them—reveling in it, writhing in it, and finally surrendering to it. Jenny cried out her passion into the dark of the night. It was a wild, sweet cry, filled with the depths of the yearning in her heart.

Later, much later, when the moon had slipped behind a wisp of a cloud, she lay with her head nestled against his chest, her body molded against his. Her thoughts were pleasantly disconnected, but she murmured to him sleepily, "Ryan. . . ?"

"Mmmm," he answered lazily.

"Your land . . ."

"What about it?"

"What *are* you going to do with it?"

He smiled in the darkness. "I don't know. Probably nothing at all."

The morning rays of the sun threw a brilliant glare against the side of their tent, shooting a tiny series of rainbows through the beads of dew that had formed on the canvas. Jenny touched it tentatively, running her finger along so that the drops collected and ran down the tent in a little stream. She was incredibly rested, reveling in a sense of well-being she had been missing for a long time. It seemed strange that only a few days ago she had been bored and restless, and now there was a new feeling of contentment that made waking up in the morning a joy. She couldn't even quite remember why she had ever been restless, and the sight of Ryan's face softened in sleep put all thoughts of it out of her mind. She felt as if she had known him for a very long time, as if he had always been there. Had it only been ten days since she had seen him sitting on that rock? She smiled a little to herself. Did it matter?

When she looked down at him again, his eyes were open. He looked utterly peaceful, and his eyes were a very clear bright blue. "Look at the sun," she greeted him. "It's glorious. This time you don't have to see it from an office window in downtown Manhattan."

He leaned over obligingly and unzipped the front of the tent, poking his head out. The sun was shining proudly behind the tops of the trees, painting the river with fresh new light. He soaked up the sight and then fell back, catching Jenny in his arms and holding her close.

"Come on . . ." She laughed, struggling to sit up. "I think I smell breakfast on the wind."

They dressed and packed up the tent, then stepped across the little island to see early-morning risers up and about at the camp on the riverbank. A lone figure was sitting on a boulder at the side of the river, and Jenny recognized Margie's silhouette. Jenny hesitated, but then Margie saw her and waved.

They paddled their canoe across the river and got out. Tank was organizing breakfast, and Jenny realized how hungry she was. The tantalizing aromas of fresh coffee, sizzling sausages, and scrambled eggs lingered invitingly in the moist, cool air. People were milling around the fire, enjoying the early-morning quiet.

Ryan went to get a cup of coffee, and Jenny stepped cautiously over to Margie and said hello. "How are you doing, Margie?" she asked.

Margie smiled. "Oh, I'm fine, Jen. Really. Please don't worry about me."

"Are you sure?"

"Oh, yes. I'm glad I found out about him when I did," Margie said emphatically. "I'm too angry to feel hurt." Her face lit up with her old vitality. "And look at this." She fished in the pocket of her windbreaker and produced a ragged piece of paper. "It's for Ryan."

"Who's it from?" Jenny frowned, eyeing it curiously.

"From him. Lester."

"Lester!" Jenny looked around, suddenly aware that she hadn't seen him. "Where is he?"

"He's gone. He left late last night." Margie was

clearly enjoying imparting this information, and Jenny was glad to see her that way.

"How did he get out of here?" Jenny asked.

Margie shrugged. "Who cares. He probably walked up to the highway and got a ride."

"Oh." Well, events had not stopped rolling while she and Ryan had been making love under the stars.

Margie called to Ryan and he strolled over, sipping at his coffee. "This is for you," she said. "From Lester."

"From Lester?" Ryan was clearly surprised, and he unfolded the paper and read it curiously. "Well, I'll be darned," he said, beginning to chuckle.

"What is it?" Jenny asked avidly. He handed her the paper and she read it aloud. " ' I, Lester Akins . . .' " She stopped. "What happened to the 'T. K.'?"

"Oh, that's not his real name," Ryan said, waving his hand. "He made up the 'T. K.' part. Read on."

" 'I, Lester Akins, hereby agree to sell the ten thousand acreas of land I have inherited from my grandfather, Josiah Akins, to my brother, Ryan Powers, for the price of one hundred dollars per acre.' " The note was signed and witnessed by two people—Margie and Tank.

Jenny laughed delighted. "What on earth possessed him to do this?"

"Oh, I don't know," Margie said impishly. "But it might have had something to do with a long-distance phone call I was thinking of making . . . to Houston." Jenny's eyes widened, and Ryan laughed. "Besides," she continued, "he knew he would never be able to do anything with the land anyway."

Jenny examined the piece of paper. "Is this legal?" she said to Ryan.

"Sure." He grinned. "It's not too fancy, but it will do. I'll send him a more formal document later on. I'm not going to give him an argument, for once."

Tank called to them from the fire, "If you folks are hungry, you'd better come and get it!" Margie smiled and ran over. She helped dish out the food as Jenny turned seriously to Ryan.

"You always knew about him, didn't you?"

He nodded. "Ever since I can remember. And he wasn't the first. Unfortunately, he took after our father."

Jenny couldn't hide her surprise. "Oh, no!"

"My father created a minor scandal in Great Barrington by romancing all the women in town. It was very embarrassing for my mother, to say the least. In a small town like that, everyone knew, and she couldn't take it. Finally she left, right after I was born. But old Josiah didn't like that. He thought that a woman's place was with her husband, no matter what he did." He paused. "Soon after that, Dad took Lester to Texas."

Jenny nodded thoughtfully. "Is that why you never saw your grandfather all those years?"

"Partly. The anger and disgust were mutual for a long time. When he died, I finally saw Lester. I was very anxious to know him, but things got off to a bad start, to put it mildly. He wanted to do things with that land that were not only unpleasant, but illegal." He sighed, but much of the bitterness was gone. "I guess I was blind to it for a while. I was so glad to have a brother."

Jenny took his hand sympathetically. "That's the real reason you came up here last week, isn't it?"

"Exactly," he confirmed. "I went over that will a hundred times, looking for some kind of loophole. It drove me crazy. I ended up here, lost in the middle of something I had never had. And the first person I met after that was you." He looked into her face with a gentleness that she had never seen in him before.

Jenny was too pleased somehow to say anything just then, and Margie was calling to them. "Come on," she said softly, squeezing his hand, "let's eat."

Hours later, they were gliding down a serene, glassy part of the river, and occasional houses were beginning to appear near the banks. They were heading closer and closer to Great Barrington on the last lap of the trip. Jenny sat back and drank in the last of the peaceful atmosphere, letting Ryan steer. They hadn't spoken much all morning, but there was an invisible, almost tangible feeling between them that she wanted to prolong. It was a delicious feeling of anticipation, and although she didn't quite know what it was leading to, she savored it and let it hang temptingly in the air. They were the last canoe in the line and she sat up when she perceived that the trip was almost over.

"I want you to say yes to something." Ryan spoke suddenly, with the old, impatient glint in his eye.

She was startled. "What? Now?"

"Of course now. You owe me one, remember?"

"Well . . ." She frowned a little, unwilling to cooperate. She didn't want to break the delicate mood that had lingered all morning. "All right," she said reluctantly.

"Are you ready?" he seemed excited.

"Yes, I'm ready. Go ahead."

There was a pause, and then he asked her point-blank. "Will you marry me?"

"What?"

"You heard me," he continued. "I asked you to marry me, and you've already said yes."

"Now, wait a minute," she protested, scarcely believing him. "That's not fair."

"Of course it's fair." He refused to be budged. "You owed me a yes. I said yes to your question, didn't I?"

"Well . . . well, yes, but . . . but what I asked you was perfectly harmless."

"This is harmless."

She blinked, and couldn't think of a thing to say. He was scrutinizing her carefully, and suddenly his face changed.

"Well, look," he said hastily. "If you don't want to, just forget it. I don't mean to force you."

She was thoroughly confused. "I didn't say I didn't want to!"

"Oh!" He brightened. "Then you do want to?"

"I . . . I . . ."

"You don't love me, right?" he interrupted calmly. Then he sighed. "I knew it."

Jenny was floored. She did love him, but now she didn't know how to tell him. Besides, he hadn't said anything about love himself. "I . . . I only scored twenty-two on the love test," she floundered.

"What? What are you talking about?"

"A love test in a magazine," she said faintly, wondering what she was talking about herself. "Ask Margie."

"All right," he said obligingly, "I will." He called

up ahead to Margie, who was now sharing a canoe with Tank. "Oh, Margie!" Margie turned around. "Did Jenny pass her love test?" His voice was perfectly serious, but his eyes were laughing. The other members of the group turned around and looked at them curiously.

"Yes, she did!" Margie called back merrily, getting right into his spirit.

"But I only got twenty-two," Jenny reminded them.

"No, you didn't," Margie said. "I looked at your answers after you left, and you added wrong, as usual. You didn't get twenty-two. You got twenty-eight! Do you know what that means?"

"No," said Jenny weakly. "What?"

"You're in love!" Margie concluded triumphantly.

Everyone laughed, and Ryan looked at Jenny. "There," he said, "you see?"

Her eyes lowered, and he threw his paddle into the canoe, letting it drift. When she looked up, he was still staring at her, but his eyes were gentle and her own eyes were asking the question that she couldn't ask aloud.

"Rock up ahead, everyone!" Tank called suddenly. The line of canoes began to veer to the right, but Jenny and Ryan weren't listening. Their canoe drifted pleasantly down with the current, and as they were staring at each other, it collided neatly with a large and familiar rock.

The bow of the canoe was edged inside a cleft in the rock, and they stopped short. Ryan looked up delightedly. "Look!" he exclaimed. "Look where we are!"

It was the same rock on which he had been perched the day they had met. Jenny's face lit up in recognition.

"Come here," he ordered her, standing up in the canoe.

"What are you doing?"

He climbed deftly onto the rock and sat down, looking immensely pleased with himself. "Come here." He held out his hand.

Something told her to do as he said, and she clambered up, gripping tightly to his hand. He put his arms around her and held her safely.

"Now," he said, "that's better. This is where my life began again. This is where I met you, and this is where I fell in love with you."

Her eyes closed for a fraction of a second. "What did you say?"

"I love you, Jenny," he repeated quietly. "Ever since I saw you standing over there. You walked into my life and I don't ever want you to leave it."

"Oh, Ryan . . ."

"You don't have to say yes right away, if you don't mean it," he went on earnestly. "But I have a lot of patience."

Her eyes crinkled. "No, you don't. You're the least patient person I've ever met."

"Is that so?"

"Yes. So I guess I'll just have to say yes right now." She turned to him, her face radiant with love. "And I do want to, Ryan. Somehow during this past crazy week, I fell in love with you too."

He kissed her slowly, almost reverently. "Are you sure?" he asked, but she knew she didn't have to answer. "You really want to spend your life with a rough-and-tumble New Yorker like me?"

She smiled. "Of course. I want to be one, remember?" But she pointed up to the hills, to the little patch of land that Lester had cleared. "And you see that space up there?" He nodded. "We can build a summer house there, and use it when city life threatens to bury us."

His arms tightened around her."I knew you'd think of something like that. That's why I need you—to keep the balance in my life. I came up here looking for a family that never was. But I found one anyway, didn't I?"

Jenny was deeply touched, but she managed to whisper, "Yes. Right here on this rock."

TELL US YOUR OPINIONS AND RECEIVE A FREE COPY OF THE RAPTURE NEWSLETTER.

Thank you for filling out our questionnaire. Your response to the following questions will help us to bring you more and better books. In appreciation of your help we will send you a free copy of the Rapture Newsletter.

1. Book Title: ______________________________

   Book #: ____________________ (5–7)

2. Using the scale below how would you rate this book on the following features? Please write in one rating from 0–10 for each feature in the spaces provided. Ignore bracketed numbers.

(Poor) 0 1 2 3 4 5 6 7 8 9 10 (Excellent)

	0–10 Rating	
Overall Opinion of Book.	________	(8)
Plot/Story.	________	(9)
Setting/Location.	________	(10)
Writing Style.	________	(11)
Dialogue.	________	(12)
Love Scenes.	________	(13)
Character Development:		
Heroine:.	________	(14)
Hero:.	________	(15)
Romantic Scene on Front Cover.	________	(16)
Back Cover Story Outline	________	(17)
First Page Excerpts.	________	(18)

3. What is your: Education: Age: ______ (20-22)

   High School ( )1 4 Yrs. College ( )3
   2 Yrs. College ( )2 Post Grad ( )4 (23)

4. Print Name: ______________________________

   Address: ______________________________

   City: ____________ State: ________ Zip: ________

   Phone # ( ) ____________________ (25)

Thank you for your time and effort. Please send to New American Library, Rapture Romance Research Department, 1633 Broadway, New York, NY 10019.

Provocative and sensual, passionate and tender— the magic and mystery of love in all its many guises

Coming next month

SEPTEMBER SONG by Lisa Moore. Swearing her career came first, Lauren Rose faced the challenge of her life in Mark Landrill's arms, for she had to choose between the work she thrived on—and a passion that left her both fulfilled and enslaved . . .

A MOUNTAIN MAN by Megan Ashe. For Kelly March, Josh Munroe's beloved mountain world was a haven where she could prove her independence. but Josh—who tormented her with desire—resented the intrusion. Could Kelly prove she was worth his love—and, if she did, would she lose all she'd fought to achieve?

THE KNAVE OF HEARTS by Estelle Edwards. Brilliant young lawyer Kate Sewell had no defense against carefree riverboat gambler Hal Lewis. But could Kate risk her career—even for the ecstasy his love promised?

BEYOND ALL STARS by Melinda McKenzie. For astronaut Ann Lafton, working with Commander Ed Saber brought emotional chaos that jeopardized their NASA shuttle mission. But Ann couldn't stop dreaming that this sensuous lover would fly her to the stars . . .

DREAMLOVER by JoAnn Robb. Painter K.L. Michaels needed Hunter St. James to pull off a daring masquerade, but she didn't count on losing her relaxed lifestyle as their wild love affair unfolded. Could their nights of sensual fireworks make up for their daily battles?

A LOVE SO FRESH by Marilyn Davids. Loving Ben Heron was everything Anna Markham needed. But she considered marriage a trap, and Ben, too, had been burned before. Passion drew them together, but was their rapture enough to overcome the obstacles they faced?

SPECIAL $1.00 REBATE OFFER WHEN YOU BUY FOUR RAPTURE ROMANCES

To receive your cash refund, send:

1. This coupon: To qualify for the $1.00 refund, this coupon, completed with your name and address, must be used. (Certificate may not be reproduced)

2. Proof of purchase: Print, on the reverse side of this coupon, the *title* of the books, the *numbers* of the books (on the upper right hand of the front cover preceding the price), and the U.P.C. numbers (on the back covers) on your next four purchases.

3. Cash register receipts, with prices circled to:
   Rapture Romance $1.00 Refund Offer
   P.O. Box NB037
   El Paso, Texas 79977

Offer good only in the U.S. and Canada. Limit one refund/response per household for any group of four Rapture Romance titles. Void where prohibited, taxed or restricted. Allow 6–8 weeks for delivery. Offer expires March 31, 1984.

NAME____

ADDRESS____________________________________

CITY_______________STATE________ZIP_________

SPECIAL $1.00 REBATE OFFER WHEN YOU BUY FOUR RAPTURE ROMANCES

See complete details on reverse

1. Book Title ______________________________

   Book Number 451-______________

   U.P.C. Number 7116200195-______________

2. Book Title ______________________________

   Book Number 451-______________

   U.P.C. Number 7116200195-______________

3. Book Title ______________________________

   Book Number 451-______________

   U.P.C. Number 7116200195-______________

4. Book Title ______________________________

   Book Number 451-______________

   U.P.C. Number 7116200195-______________

U.P.C. Number

0 71162 00195

SAMPLE